TERROR IN THE ATTIC

In the moonlight he saw the bare wood floor and the piles of antiques.

The attic smelled of dust and cloth and mildew.

He sat with one hand clutching the object that had gotten him in trouble in the first place.

A tin soldier.

Darn her, anyway.

Who did she think she was, putting him—a grown man—up here just because once in a while he—

But he didn't like to think about that.

The swell of a massive trunk lay before him in the shadows. Then a wooden torso form for fitting dresses.

So much junk.

Tears in his eyes, he began to play with the tin soldier.

It gleamed in the darkness, the metal bayonet deadly sharp, the face immobile and staring. It didn't like it up here in the attic any better than he did. Oh no, it didn't like it one little bit.

And this time she would have to suffer the consequences, once and for all. . . .

THRILLERS & CHILLERS
from Zebra Books

DADDY'S LITTLE GIRL   (1606, $3.50)
by Daniel Ransom
Sweet, innocent Deirde was missing. But no one in the small quiet town of Burton wanted to find her. They had waited a long time for the perfect sacrifice. And now they had found it . . .

THE CHILDREN'S WARD   (1585, $3.50)
by Patricia Wallace
Abigail felt a sense of terror form the moment she was admitted to the hospital. And as her eyes took on the glow of those possessed and her frail body strengthened with the powers of evil, little Abigail—so sweet, so pure, so innocent—was ready to wreak a bloody revenge in the sterile corridors of THE CHILDREN'S WARD.

SWEET DREAMS   (1553, $3.50)
by William W. Johnstone
Innocent ten-year-old Heather sensed the chill of darkness in her schoolmates' vacant stares, the evil festering in their hearts. But no one listened to Heather's terrified screams as it was her turn to feed the hungry spirit—with her very soul!

THE NURSERY   (1566, $3.50)
by William W. Johnstone
Their fate had been planned, their master chosen. Sixty-six infants awaited birth to live forever under the rule of darkness—if all went according to plan in THE NURSERY.

SOUL-EATER   (1656, $3.50)
by Dana Brookins
The great old house stood empty, the rafter beams seemed to sigh, and the moon beamed eerily off the white paint. It seemed to reach out to Bobbie, wanting to get inside his mind as if to tell him something he didn't want to hear.

TOYS IN THE ATTIC
BY DANIEL RANSOM

ZEBRA BOOKS
KENSINGTON PUBLISHING CORP.

ZEBRA BOOKS

are published by

Kensington Publishing Corp.
475 Park Avenue South
New York, NY 10016

First printing: July 1986

Printed in the United States of America

For Terry Butler,
who fights the fight

Acknowledgement

I would like to thank Wendy McCurdy, whose good sense is matched by her good taste.

Part One

Chapter One

1

The rain began just as the two graveyard attendants stepped in past the pot-bellied priest and
started to lower the casket into the ground.

Winches and ropes and a small electric motor were
all part of the burial process, as if to remind the
children who ringed the gravesite that even death
was a mechanical matter.

The stout priest, whose belly looked like a small
planet pressed against his black robe, folded his
Bible abruptly and wiped rain from his face with a
pudgy finger. "We'd better be getting on now,
children," he said, just as a dagger of lightning
ripped down the gray morning sky.

And so they left, the children from Windhaven
Orphanage, back to the cars that had brought them,
back to their world, which was a huge refurbished
mansion on the edge of Haversham, a midwestern

town of forty thousand.

All except a twelve-year-old boy named Brian Courtney.

He remained by the gravesite, watching as the attendants finished their business.

Brian had never been this close to death before. What amazed him was how indifferent these two men were to what they were doing.

Didn't they know they were burying an eleven-year-old boy named Davie Mason, who just happened to be Brian's best friend?

They grunted and groaned with their work, the men, moving the casket into place above the earthen hole. The way they slid the big box around, Brian got the impression they were manhandling some kind of wild animal that did not want to be tamed.

A long, thin line of lightning angled outward across the gray morning. The flash startled Brian. He jerked back, as if he'd been attacked.

The attendants had been watching him. Seeing him afraid, they smiled to each other, then went back to their work.

Brian could no longer hold the tears back.

Davie Mason was dead. His roommate of the past six months. Dead. Orphans did not have a lot of continuity in their lives. Brian needed all he could get. Now the kid he'd been closest to was—dead.

He had just touched his hand to his head, to shield his eyes from the curiosity of the attendants, when a huge, dark shape wriggled free from one of the waiting cars and struggled its odd way down the hill to where Brian stood.

From even a hundred feet away it was impossible

to give the shape a sex. Dressed in a dark man's suit, with a high, somewhat old-fashioned man's collar and a dark necktie, the figure moved with a peculiar combination of grace and awkwardness that made guessing its sex even more difficult.

Then the shape, a stern six foot of it, was upon Brian.

He was unaware of Mrs. Kilrane until his ear was between her thumb and index finger and until she was twisting it so hard that he had to fall to his knees to keep from passing out.

"I thought we told you to get to the car," she snapped, rain staining her wireless glasses.

But he couldn't speak and she knew it.

The pain was too great.

She twisted again and brought him to his feet, like something writhing on the end of her finger.

And before he could recover himself from his grief over his dead friend, let alone recover from the pain her ear-twisting had caused, Mrs. Kilrane brought her hand expertly across the side of his face, with a slap that sounded like a pistol shot.

The attendants looked at each other and frowned, exchanging glances that said they were glad their own children did not have to live this way.

"Now," Mrs. Kilrane said, shoving Brian Court-ney ahead of her in the downpour, "you get back to that car, young man."

2

In the early November darkness of his room, Brian Courtney stared out of the window at the chill rain sliding down the glass and the hue of streetlight across the way.

Elsewhere in the orphanage he could hear the noise of the other kids on their way downstairs to the dining hall.

Most of them, laughing, shouting, shoving, had seemed to have forgotten all about Davie Mason.

It was less than ten hours after Davie's funeral.

Brian got up, the cot squeaking, the taste of the licorice he'd had earlier still strong in his mouth.

He wasn't hungry and didn't feel like facing people anyway.

Especially Mrs. Kilrane.

She hadn't liked him since the first day he'd come here, after being gently moved out of his foster home because the people had found him too strange.

And that was what Mrs. Kilrane had told him on his first day here. "You're in your own little world, Brian, and a lot of people resent that." Then she'd smiled. Chillingly. Her face could easily have been a man's. "I know I do."

There'd been a time when he felt he'd been getting along with Mrs. Kilrane. But now he knew better. After twisting his ear and slapping him so hard that his teeth had bitten into his upper lip, she had made her feelings unmistakably clear.

Which might not have been so bad, except that Mrs. Kilrane was the chief administrator of Windhaven.

Brian walked to the west window.

No light could be seen in its glass. Just the farm fields beyond and the swampy area that was fenced off so that kids wouldn't fall in.

Brian stood and stared, much as he had earlier this afternoon at the gravesite.

At first he wasn't sure what he was staring at—maybe just off into space—but finally he realized that his eyes had rested on the surface of the swamp itself. In the moonlight and the rain the small lake of a swamp seemed to bubble, like tar boiling.

Windhaven had been accused by some citizens' groups of having an illegal landfill right across from the orphanage—the result of a hauling firm that used to be situated right across from here thirty years ago, a firm that hadn't been bothered at all about dumping toxic waste—a landfill that endangered the lives of Windhaven's children.

At least that's what the citizens' groups said.

Windhaven had contended otherwise. So had the city council of Haversham. Which was not all that surprising, according to the talk of the older boys.

Mrs. Kilrane's father was the most powerful man in Haversham. And it had been his own father whose firm had dumped the toxic waste in the first place.

Brian continued to stare out the window, fascinated by the bubbling effect, as if it were a cauldron about to boil over.

Brian.

In the deep shadows of his room, a room smelling of disinfectant and dampness and the wool of heavy blankets, Brian looked around for the source of the sound.

Brian.

There it was again.

But before he could wonder about the source of the sound, a familiar shape appeared in the doorway.

An ominous black-clad figure.

"You're supposed to be eating."

"I guess I'm just not hungry."

"You get downstairs and eat. And right now, young man."

"But Mrs. Kilrane—"

The shape moved.

Almost supernaturally.

Crossed the room and got his ear. This time the tears were instant. This time she did not hold back at all.

She jerked and tugged on his ear until he started screaming, and when he screamed she hit him.

The same way she'd hit him that afternoon.

Then she dragged him into the hall where a burly man named Dodge, dressed as always in white tee shirt and tight white slacks, took Brian from Mrs. Kilrane, and continued the forced march down the stairs.

Around Windhaven, Dodge was popularly rumored to be "friendly" with Mrs. Kilrane. Exactly what this meant, Brian wasn't sure—but occasionally he caught glimpses of the muscular man patting Mrs. Kilrane on the butt or sliding his arm around

16

her. Dodge was the peacekeeper at Windhaven—if you got out of line, he quickly got you back into it.

"You really piss her off, kid," Dodge laughed. "You better watch yourself or she's really gonna make your life tough."

Dodge seemed to be enjoying the hell out of himself.

Brian puked up his dinner.

Usually vomiting scared him—he was always afraid he was going to strangle—but tonight he had no choice.

The day—Davie's funeral, his two confrontations with Mrs. Kilrane, the loneliness that overwhelmed him from time to time, and overwhelmed him now—had made him sick to his stomach.

When he got back to his room from the john, Mr. Rydell was waiting for him.

Mr. Rydell worked for Mrs. Kilrane. The short, slight man with the wispy mustache and the cigarette-yellowed teeth was a counselor here at the orphanage.

Mr. Rydell said, "You've got it again, don't you?" He held up the framed photograph of a pretty woman in her early thirties. Her gentle brown eyes and subtly smiling mouth spoke of kindness and tenderness.

Brian said nothing. Only shuddered so hard he was afraid he'd snap a bone.

"You don't need to be afraid of me," Mr. Rydell said. "Aren't we friends?"

Brian disliked Mr. Rydell almost as much as he did Mrs. Kilrane. She hit you—which hurt, but at least he understood what she was doing. But Mr. Rydell was always talking in his too-sweet voice, and always touching you. Always.

"Why don't you come over here, Brian?"

"Is it okay if I stay over here, Mr. Rydell?"

"My," Mr. Rydell said. In the harsh lamplight—the linen shade long ago stained with soda pop—Mr. Rydell's teeth seemed even yellower. "You're a very shy boy, aren't you?" He looked at Brian and smiled. "You're a lot like me, I'll bet."

That last sentence seemed to have some special significance for Mr. Rydell because he let it hang in the air for a long time.

"Come here and take a closer look at this photograph, Brian."

Mr. Rydell was still trying to get him to come closer. Brian stood unmoving. "Then stay there and answer my question. Who is this woman?"

"My mother."

Mr. Rydell sighed again. As if he were a very, very weary man.

"Brian," he said, "you know better than that. You know much, much better than that."

Brian said nothing.

"What if I were to tell Mrs. Kilrane? Would you like that?"

Brian still said nothing.

"I said, Brian, would you like that?"

"No, sir."

"Then once and for all get rid of this picture."

"She's my mother, Mr. Rydell."

With that, the older man did something he seemed quite unaccustomed to doing.

Jumped from the bed, and in a cold hard rage, took

the framed photograph and smashed the whole thing against the iron bedpost.

Glass shattered; the gold-sprayed metal of the frame bent in half; the photograph fell listlessly to the floor.

Then Mr. Rydell turned on Brian and said, "How do you think it makes me look in front of Mrs. Kilrane, young man? She ordered me to get rid of that photo two weeks ago."

Because he wasn't afraid of Mr. Rydell, Brian knelt down on the floor and picked the photograph up. There was a place where the shattered glass had cut through the woman's left cheek. Like a knife.

Brian felt dead inside.

Mr. Rydell was in a frenzy again, leaning in and shouting in his face. "You bought that photo at K-Mart a month ago! She's nothing more than a model and you're just pretending that she's your mother! Just pretending—do you hear me?"

With that, he tore the photograph from Brian's hands and ripped it in half. Then he ripped it in fourths.

Brian only watched.

Mr. Rydell was right, of course. He had bought the photo at K-Mart. The woman was a model whose picture came free with the cheap wire frame.

But it didn't matter.

For a few weeks Brian had had a mother. Or at least a picture of one. And he kept her photo right on his bureau.

At least until one of the other boys on the floor had told Mrs. Kilrane, who in turn had told Mr. Rydell.

"Now," Mr. Rydell was saying, "I want you to

pick up those pieces of the photograph and bring them with me into the restroom. Do you understand?"

Brian nodded. Numb.

Three minutes later he stood next to Mr. Rydell over one of the wash basins in the restroom.

"Put them in the sink."

Brian did as Mr. Rydell instructed.

"Here."

Mr. Rydell handed Brian a book of matches. "Now I want you to burn the pieces. Burn them right in front of me."

Mr. Rydell was apparently taking no chances. Last time he'd merely thrown the photo out in the garbage. Brian had found it and brought it back to his room.

He wouldn't be doing that this time.

"Go ahead, Brian. Get it over with."

Brian raised the matches. Tore one off. Struck it. Set it against the pieces of photographic paper.

Now the tears came.

"She was my mother," he said quietly to Mr. Rydell. "She was my mother."

All Mr. Rydell did was shake his head sadly and try to slide his arm around Brian.

Brian jerked away.

4

In the distant night there were trucks. Brian dreamed of being on one, roaring through the darkness toward places with exotic names such as New Mexico and Arizona and Wyoming.

Anyplace, as a matter of fact, but Windhaven.

A while ago he'd gotten up and checked the luminous face of his Timex wristwatch. After midnight.

Mrs. Kilrane would be very angry if she knew he was up at this hour. She inspected everybody's eyes in the morning and at breakfast and if they looked tired, then she got very mad and accused them of reading under the covers or even far worse things.

After midnight.

There had been a time in his life when midnight had held the same magic sound as Arizona or New Mexico for Brian. He associated the hour, in a delicious sort of way, with spooks and goblins.

No more.

After midnight simply meant feeling tired and far lonelier than you could ever feel during daylight hours.

After midnight brought back murky memories of the mother who'd given him up when he was four— his father already long gone—the mother with the braids and the Grateful Dead t-shirt and funny-smelling cigarettes, whose real nature Brian now knew—the mother who gave him up to be a ward of the state because she could no longer "cope" (a word that caused him pain every time he heard or saw it, his memories so bitter).

After midnight meant hearing the way the orphanage made noises—plumbing and shine roof and creaking wood—the way an old person struggling to live made noises.

After midnight.

If only he were back with his mother again, and the prospect of midnight were still fun.

He lay there with his hands behind his head staring at the ceiling. Just staring. The way he had at the gravesite today. Into the shadowy recesses of the grave itself.

What was it like to be dead?

Did Davie, this afternoon, look up and watch everybody standing over his grave?

Brian was thinking this when he heard the sound again.

The sound he'd heard earlier.

Brian.

He jerked up in bed. His eyes searched the darkness for a glimpse of anybody who could be calling his name.

But there was nothing.

Somehow he managed to struggle back to sleep once more. But around two he woke up again.

He wasn't sure what woke him. The wind, most likely. It rattled the windows like cats clawing sheet metal.

He sat up. Looked around.

Brian.

This time he got out of bed.

For a moment he couldn't move. Was paralyzed. He had to pee and he had to scream but he couldn't do either. He stood there watching the shadows play deep across the room and looking at the closet door that was slightly ajar.

Brian.

He shuddered. Maybe it was coming from the closet. He imagined eyes in the gloom inside—eyes patient and evil as anything concocted in a monster movie. Eyes that were watching him . . . waiting for him.

The windows rattled and his head whipped around. Instantly he was sure he had just made a fatal mistake in taking his eyes off the closet door. He whipped his head back again, his heart in his throat. But nothing had changed.

Finally he moved. One foot at a time. Toward the closet door. In his ears his heartsounds were huge, hammering. He said "God damnit" to himself then immediately regretted taking the Lord's name in vain. What a time to piss off God.

His hand reached out tentatively in the darkness and found the knob on the closet door. Easy to imagine the slavering jaws of a monster opening now—

He flung the door back. There in the light from the window, was—nothing.

Except for shoes and a ball bat, the closet was empty.

Brian.

His name again, whispered urgently. He backed away from the closet. His heart still hammering, he checked under the bed. Nothing.

Brian.

By now there was only one place left to look. Outside the window.

For a long moment he thought he'd figured it out. Obviously it was somebody standing out on the ledge next to his window. Calling his name in as spooky a voice as possible. Just to scare him.

The trouble with that theory struck him almost at once.

Who was going to stand out on a ledge all night in a chilling November downpour? Not even the bullies at Windhaven had that kind of nerve or patience.

He went to the window and peered through the rain silvered by the moonlight at the fenced-in area near the swamp.

The room still danced with shadow and mystery.

He still had the vague but unmistakable impression that he was trapped inside a nightmare. Soon he'd wake up and . . .

Brian—

Somehow the voice was even louder now. The sound of his name had taken on a sing-song dimension, like the neat video of Motely Crue he'd once seen on MTV. Yeah, he thought, that was what this whole thing was like, sort of like a video on MTV, with the smoke bombs swirling fog and something spooky—that you couldn't quite make out—on the other side of the fog.

Brian.

But then again, who was he kidding? It wasn't anything like MTV at all, because MTV didn't make his throat dry up and sweat fill up his armpits.

Through the murk of rain and fog, he saw it. A bluish glow, right in the center of the swampy area. He rubbed his tired eyes and moved so close to the window that his nose pressed the cold pane. The blue glow was there all right. Every few minutes it seemed to throb—like an emergency warning light, only much fainter. All Brian could think of was that he sure as hell wished this was only MTV.

Brian found a yellow rain slicker in the closet, found buckle galoshes nearby and put them on. Then he started the long and dangerous process of sneaking out of the orphanage.

6

"You're working kinda late tonight, aren't you, Sheriff?"

The sheriff of Haversham County looked up and smiled. Glanced up at the General Electric clock on the wall and nodded a weary head. "Guess I am, at that."

Deputy Farnsworth came further into the large, well-organized room with its bank of computers on the west wall and its line of filing cabinets on the other. Farnsworth was a mild man, even meek, surprising in a law officer, even more surprising in someone his size. He stood six-two, and at the county fair always took first place in the arm-wrestling contest.

He went over to the Mr. Coffee, picked up the pot, and said, "I could go for another pot, how about you?"

"Fine," Sheriff Baines said. And went back to the file on the desk.

Sheriff Baines was only peripherally aware of the deputy over the next ten minutes. Baines had come upon something in the fifteen-year-old files under scrutiny.

"Here," Farnsworth said and put a steaming mug of coffee down on the edge of the sheriff's desk.

Baines looked up. Smiled gratefully. "Thanks."

Farnsworth stood by, unmoving. Obviously he wanted to say something. Baines wasn't sure what.

Farnsworth kind of cleared his throat, and kind of shuffled his feet, and kind of put a sappy grin on his face. "I'd like to say something, Sheriff."

"Well, go ahead, Deputy. Say what's on your mind."

"Well."

Baines glanced back at the files to indicate that there was much work to do. "I'm really in sort of a hurry, Deputy."

"Well," Farnsworth said. "What I wanted to say was—well, I like your new hair style very much."

Sheriff Diane Baines let a big smile part her lips as she looked at the large, clumsy deputy with a mixture of frustration and fondness. "You still can't get used to it, can you, Bill?"

He smiled. "I guess it's kind of hard for me, I mean, if we're being honest here."

"We're being honest here."

"It's just that over the past fifteen years, I mean all the time I've been a deputy, I guess I just got used to Sheriff Moore. His way of doing things."

The smile lingered on Diane Baines' face. But now there was a hint of sadness in it, too. An MA in criminology. Five years on one of the toughest urban police forces in the state. Two commendations for excellence as an officer. And she still had to confront this kind of sexism. In Farnsworth's case, however, it was an almost innocent kind of sexism. He liked her, even respected her. Indeed, he seemed to have no problem accepting her as his superior officer and a highly qualified sheriff. Nor did he apparently have

any difficulty in seeing her as an attractive woman—
she was five-six, with honey-blond hair and an
angular face almost luminous with melancholy and
a body kept in shape, at thirty-six, by running three
miles a day. Farnsworth's problem seemed to be that
he could not accept her as both. Farnsworth had had
this problem since she'd first come here three years
ago, fleeing from a husband who'd just announced
that he was in love with somebody else and a doctor
who had pronounced her infertile. She'd only been a
deputy then, just like Farnsworth, but now she was
both the woman he was "sweet on," as locals phrased
it, and his boss. For Bill Farnsworth, a heck of a nice
guy as she well knew, this was a big dilemma.

"Thanks for the coffee and the compliment," she
said.

"You bet," Farnsworth grinned, flushing.

He looked as if he wanted to be anywhere in the
world right now but right here.

He turned to go.

She said, "Bill, do you remember anything about a
boy from Windhaven being struck in a hit-and-run
accident about fifteen years ago?"

He turned back, obviously relieved that they were
going to talk about business.

"Fifteen years ago," he said, calculating the time
in his mind. "Oh, that would have been right after I
got back from Nam."

Bill Farnsworth had been an early enlistee in the
Viet Nam struggle. By the time his tour was over he'd
risen to corporal and been decorated for bravery, and
he resolutely refused to talk about his experiences
there. Whatever his feelings on the subject, he kept

29

them to himself.

"Afraid I don't remember it," he said. "Why?"

"I don't know."

"That why you came down here so late tonight? The death of that kid out at Windhaven a couple of days ago?"

She got up, looking trim in her white blouse and designer jeans, and picked up her sweater from the back of her chair. She turned around and stared out the window. Rain still lashed the building. The moon could be seen only through sheets of silver rain and drifting fog.

"I just sense something not being right," she said.

"It was pretty simple," Farnsworth replied. "The kid just fell down the steps a few days ago and broke his neck. He got up late at night and apparently was walking in his sleep, and just took a tumble. There were three different witnesses."

"Yes," Diane Baines said softly, "and all three of them are Windhaven employees."

Farnsworth's brow pinched. "You saying they aren't telling the truth?"

"I'm just saying I'd feel better if one of the witnesses were a kid."

"But why would you doubt the witnesses, especially when one of them is related to—" The full implications of Diane's statement finally struck him.

"Exactly," she said. Her tone was not without bitterness. "How could I doubt the witnesses when one of them is related to Raymond Stockbridge."

Raymond Stockbridge had dominated Haversham politics since just after World War II. During the war, the US Government had turned his otherwise

30

small-time construction company into a giant, retaining it to build air strips and hangars for secret government projects throughout the Midwest. Stockbridge had taken advantage of the situation by building up hundreds of acres of land in and near Haversham. Today he and his cronies virtually ran the small city like a fiefdom, employing dozens of their relatives in various city jobs. Windhaven Orphanage alone listed half a dozen Stockbridge relatives on the payroll.

"Are you calling them liars?"

She smiled, trying to lighten the moment. "Just doing my job, Bill. That's all."

His face got a familiar look of protectiveness on it. Bill Farnsworth was the human equivalent of a St. Bernard. "I just don't want to see you get into any trouble, Sheriff."

She looked at him fondly. "You can always start calling me Diane, Bill. I won't demote you. I promise."

He flushed. "You know how the Stockbridges are; that's all I meant. You start asking questions about them, and even though you're sheriff—"

"I know, and I appreciate your concern." She lifted the coffee mug to her lips and sipped at the burning liquid. "You worked with Sheriff Tyler for a few years."

Farnsworth looked curious. "Sure. Why?"

"How did he get along with the Stockbridges?"

"All right, I guess." The curiosity had not yet left his tone.

"He was sheriff fifteen years ago when this hit-and-run accident took place. I thought maybe I'd

31

look him up. You know where I could find him?"

"He's a security guard, last I heard, out at the private air strip on the edge of town. You really going to look him up?"

"Yes. Isn't that all right?"

"It's just what we were talking about, is all. How the Stockbridges wouldn't like it."

She smiled with more pleasure than she felt. "Wouldn't it be nice in this town to do something once that the Stockbridges *didn't* like?"

"The election's only a year off—"

He was right about that. The election was coming up soon enough. She'd gotten the sheriff's job only when the sheriff who'd hired her had fallen dead from a heart attack. The Stockbridges on the County Commissioners' board had only appointed her because they'd felt it would be a good public relations gesture to make a woman sheriff. But her support in Haversham was thin and she knew it.

She went back to the window. Rain whipped the naked black trees and wind rocked the cars parked in the errie light of the mercury vapors. She hugged her arms, feeling a familiar sense of isolation. It was time to start dating again, she knew, and certainly she was tempted to tell Bill Farnsworth that anytime he wanted to take her out to dinner, he should feel free. But she knew instinctively that she was not the kind of woman he needed—he had been divorced himself a few years back from a woman he hinted had become too "modern" for him to deal with—and her sense of things was that any romantic relationship between the two of them would be doomed from the start.

"You sure you want to pursue this?" Farnsworth asked.

She had been so lost in her own thoughts that for a moment she thought Bill was referring to their own possible relationship instead of the Stockbridge matter.

Then she realized what he meant and said, "Yes, I'm sure."

"You really don't think that Davie Mason died the way three different witnesses said he did?"

She looked at him soberly and said, very simply, "No, I don't."

Chapter Two

1

The wind was like walking into a wall.

Several times on his way to the swampy area, Brian Courtney had to fall against a tree and hold on unless he wanted to be knocked to the ground.

Wind, rain, fog combined to give him the impression that he was walking deep into a netherworld that became more insubstantial the longer he went on.

He could not see Windhaven now. It was lost completely in the haze.

Even the swampy area eluded his gaze—all he had to guide him was the voice—*Brian*—that cried out but remained as insubstantial as this world itself.

By the time his hand reached out and felt the cold metal strands of fencing surrounding the swampy area, his face had been chafed raw. His shoes squished, his slicker was freezing cold on the outside, and on the inside steamed from his sweat. His nose ran and his bladder (which he should have emptied before he left) felt like the size of a wiffle ball.

Brian.

But he kept moving ahead, drawn by the voice.

He put a hand on one of the poles that protruded from the fence every ten feet or so and then climbed over. It seemed easy until, one leg on the other side of the fence, he got his slicker caught. He had to tug and rip at the slicker material until it tore in half. Then he tumbled to the ground on the inside of the fence.

Blinded by the elements, he could see nothing. Only his fingers told him of the differences between this side of the fence and the other.

The ground here did not quite feel like normal ground. There was a slimy feeling to it, as if his hand had slipped into a jar of Vaseline.

He scrambled to his feet, the wind doing its best to keep him flat to the ground, and saw again the bluish glow in the swampy area.

Brian.

For the first time, now that he was close to the swamp, he recognized the voice.

It was his friend Davie Mason who'd died a few days ago.

Fighting the treacherous night, trying not to slip on the oozing ground, he made his way to the edge of the swamp.

The bluish light glowed even deeper.

Then, oddly, he lost awareness of the ravaging elements. As if something had commanded them to stop in a small area directly around him.

He stood there, more calmly now, a slightly built

twelve-year-old boy in a yellow rain slicker with several patches on its backside, and watched as the light in the swamp grew deeper and broader.

And then he heard the voice.

A muted, terrifying sound, like the roar in his head whenever he imagined getting even with Mrs. Kilrane and the indifferent community who let her get away with everything—someday, he often daydreamed, he would set fire to Windhaven, destroy the whole town. . . .

Above the furious wind, timed to the pulsations of the pulsating blue glow that troubled the surface of the swamp, came Davie Mason's voice.

Brian.

Help me.

2

"And just where were you last night, young man?"

Mrs. Kilrane had not even given him a chance to wake up.

She'd simply shaken him from his exhaustion and flung his mud-covered clothes in his face.

It hadn't taken any brilliant deductions on her part to realize that somebody had gone out last night.

Brian remembered tracking mud into the orphanage and all the way upstairs, but being too tired to do anything about it.

"You know where you're going this morning, don't you, young man?"

But before he could speak, or even think, she leaned in and slapped his face with such force that she knocked his head back against the wall.

For several long moments he was unconscious, and when he came to, Mrs. Kilrane did something not altogether unexpected for a woman like herself.

She slapped him again with equal ferocity.

3

Breakfast tasted good this morning. Eggs, bacon, toast with jam.

Brian sat near the back of the dining room, where the two fat cooks, dripping sweat, sat smoking Kools and gossiping about things they'd read in a recent *Enquirer.* Brian had heard these two men talk before. They had very severe opinions about TV stars, especially the virtue of the female stars. These women divided evenly into two camps, "goddamn bitches" or "goddamn real ladies." There didn't seem to be any in-between.

Brian had taken two aspirins. His head still throbbed from where Mrs. Kilrane had pounded it.

He sat there overhearing the conversation of the two cooks—it was getting kind of interesting now, them speculating on who was going to be a certain often-married star's next husband—when he looked up and saw Caroline standing a few feet away staring at him.

Even the sight of her brought back the sadness he'd been feeling lately.

Caroline, whom he'd considered his girlfriend, the only confidante he'd had in the whole world other than Davie Mason, had been adopted.

In another two weeks she would be leaving for Des Moines, where her adoptive parents lived in a big house near a lake.

Caroline Hayes came over.

"Hi," she said.

"Hi."

"You still mad?"

"Huh-uh."

"You sound like you are."

"I'm not."

"May I sit down?"

Her use of the word "may" almost made him smile. She had taught him the difference between "may" and "can." Most people always said "can I" do such-and-such. They were wrong. Caroline was not only very pretty in her braided pigtails and her jeans and sweaters, she was also smart.

She sat down across from him. He felt his usual mixture of adoration and misery whenever he was around Caroline. Adoration because she was the nicest, prettiest girl he had ever known, and misery because he had always known their friendship was too good to be true.

"You already got in trouble with Mrs. Kilrane this morning," Caroline said in a low voice.

He nodded.

"You've really got to be careful, Brian."

"I know."

"The kids said you tried to run away, that's why she got so mad." Her blue eyes were wide with concern. "Did you really try to run away?"

"No."

"So how come you tried to leave the building last night?"

Brian sighed, looked up at her. He wanted to tell

her, but was not sure he should.

He thought of what had happened at the swamp last night. He wondered now if he hadn't imagined most of it.

He hoped so.

He hoped that what he feared was real actually wasn't. . . .

She must have seen how the tension gripped his body and how his right hand began to twitch.

"What's the matter?" she said.

But when she reached out to tug on his sleeve, he jumped up and fled the dining room.

4

An hour later a shiny black limousine pulled up in front of Windhaven.

A brown-skinned man with crinkling gray hair got out of the driver's door, walked the considerable distance back to the rear of the massive vehicle, then opened the door.

A size fourteen shoe, very black and very shiny, set foot on the concrete. This was followed by the rubber tip of a fat cane. Then another very black and very shiny shoe appeared on the pavement, the cuffed trousers of a blue suit touching the laces of the shoe.

The massive man, his real size hidden inside the almost capelike folds of his dark overcoat, put out his gnarled wooden walking stick and started up the steps of Windhaven Orphanage. He gave the impression of being a very flamboyant stage actor of another era, complete with white hair, mesmerizing black eyes, and an air of utter scorn and cruelty at whatever his gaze encountered.

Brian sat watching the man's arrival.

As Mrs. Kilrane had predicted, the man had indeed arrived this morning.

The man no kid at Windhaven ever wanted to see.

Mr. Raymond Stockbridge himself.

* * *

Their meeting was in Mrs. Kilrane's office. She left the room looking very smug.

Up close, Mr. Stockbridge was even more formidable than he appeared from a distance.

He sat on a straight-backed chair across the simple, tidy office from Brian. He leaned forward on his cane, still lost in the dark billows of his coat. With his savage beak of a nose, his red, flushed complexion, and the dark accusing glare of his eyes, he resembled nothing less than an eagle. The patriarch of all eagles.

Brian knew that he was Mrs. Kilrane's father, but he could see no resemblance whatsoever. None. And he thought this very odd.

"Now then," Mr. Stockbridge intoned, in a voice worthy of his looks, a deep, rumbling, intimidating baritone, "I'm told you ran away last night."

"N-no, sir."

"Are you calling my daughter a liar?" Mr. Stockbridge's voice said that Brian had better not be.

"N-no, sir."

"Then what are you saying, young man?"

"I—I just went for a walk."

"A walk? After midnight? When it was pouring down rain?"

Brian nodded.

Mr. Stockbridge studied Brian for what seemed like six or seven hours. Just sat there, huge beyond description, leaning on his cane, staring unblinkingly at the boy.

Brian didn't know what to do except to sit and fidget and say a silent prayer that this would be over soon.

Suddenly Mr. Stockbridge leaned even closer and said, "Now I want you to tell me the truth."

"I am telling you the truth." But even as he spoke, Brian knew that his eyes betrayed him. He was neither a good nor a practiced liar.

"Where did you go last night?" Mr. Stockbridge repeated.

"For a walk."

Mr. Stockbridge's face flushed an even deeper red, a blood-purple color that seeped into his sagging jowls, even into his eyes. His eyes blazed. "You'll stand by that story, then?"

"Yes, sir."

Mr. Stockbridge surprised Brian by laughing. A laugh that seemed as big as the man himself. He could see Mr. Stockbridge shake with jollity beneath his coat.

He wondered what was going on. In all respects, Mr. Stockbridge was a strange man.

"Do you know how afraid of me most children are here at Windhaven?"

"Yes, sir."

"For thirty years most of the boys and girls at Windhaven have trembled at the mere mention of my name. Is that true?"

"Yes, sir." Brian had no idea what else to say.

"Then wouldn't it stand to reason that if I'm such a terrible figure, that a child would be afraid to lie to me because he knows that the punishment would be far beyond anything they could endure? Wouldn't that stand to reason?"

Brian nodded.

Mr. Stockbridge sat back in his chair. His air of

44

amusement still shone in his eyes.

Gray clouds rolled along a gray sky. The windows rattled with gusts of winter cold. The furnace roared in the air shaft. Mrs. Kilrane's desk was so finely organized it gave the impression of bleakness. Brian could never remember feeling more alone.

"I'm going to give you forty-eight hours, Brian."

"Forty-eight hours?"

"Yes, to think things over. To change your story, Brian. To admit to me that you're lying."

Brian said nothing. There was nothing to say. Not now.

Mr. Stockbridge put his weight on his walking stick, as if he were going to rise. Then he sank back down. His curious smile was back.

"I'd like you to come over here, Brian, and put out your hands."

Brian sighed, crossed the room. Mr. Stockbridge was not like Mr. Rydell. There was no refusing Mr. Stockbridge.

He stood in front of Mr. Stockbridge and put out his hands.

"Palms up, if you will."

Brian obeyed.

Before he had a chance even to see what was about to happen, Mr. Stockbridge brought up his gnarled cane and smashed it down hard across Brian's palms.

"Are you lying to me?" Mr. Stockbridge roared.

Tears stood in Brian's eyes. This was far more pain than Mrs. Kilrane had ever inflicted on him. His hands felt as if they were on fire. "No, sir."

Brian's words were immediately followed by Mr.

Stockbridge's thunderous laugh again. "Good for you. You're a brave boy. A formidable adversary."

Amazed, Brian felt as if he had passed some sort of mysterious test.

From the folds of his coat, Mr. Stockbridge took something that flashed metallically as he brought it up to the light.

Then he raised it to Brian's face.

"Know what this is?"

"I think so," Brian said, trying to keep the lingering tears from his voice.

"What is it?"

"A tin soldier?"

"Very good. I was raised in a very poor family, and it was all my parents could afford to give their children for Christmas. Now that I'm rich, I still haven't found anything that gives me nearly as much pleasure." He dropped the tin soldier in Brian's palm, the same palm that still burned from the cane, and pressed the palm closed with his own hand. "I've only given these to a few special boys and girls over the years." The smile shone in his eyes again. "Boys and girls who show some spunk. Who dare to challenge me. Like you, Brian."

"Yes, sir." Again, Brian felt as if he'd just been given a passing score in some strange contest.

"Now you run along and tell my daughter to come in here."

Brian nodded, got to the door as quickly as possible.

When his hand touched the doorknob, and slowly began to turn it, Mr. Stockbridge said, amusement still very much in his voice, "You remember now,

Brian. Forty-eight hours. Or you face some very severe punishment."

"Yes, sir," Brian said.

Then, without quite knowing why, he started running.

He saw Mrs. Kilrane, who looked shocked by his running, and shouted to her, "Your father wants to see you!"

Then he ran out into the hall, where in the polished vastness, his slapping footsteps echoed like gunfire.

He had never been more afraid in his life.

An hour later all you could see of Brian was his dishwater cowlick sticking up over the top of a huge volume entitled *Supernatural Visitors*. The book went into fond detail on every kind of ghost, goblin, and monster that had seemingly been known to mankind. But not a single word about voices calling to people from swamps.

So maybe he had, after all, imagined it.

Maybe he had, after all, because of what adults always called "stress," gone out into the storm last night, but had only *thought* he'd heard Davie Mason calling to him.

That was why he hadn't told Mr. Stockbridge the exact truth. Mr. Haversham would have thought that Brian was crazy, a certifiable loony. And now Brian had something new to worry about—the forty-eight hours Mr. Stockbridge had given him.

If he handed out punishment like the cane so freely, Brian did not like even to think about what Mr. Stockbridge's "real" punishment might be.

He went back to the book.

More ghosts and goblins.

But not a word about voices from swamps.

There was only one way to find out if last night's events had really taken place. He would have to go back to the swamp tonight. Only this time he would take somebody with him as a witness.

He would take Caroline.

6

Sheriff Diane Baines got out of her patrol car, touched a slender hand to the small of her back, and looked at the small, shabby cottage in front of her. With a new roof, a paint job, and a day or two spent raking the front yard, the place could be not only pleasant but downright cozy, especially given its location here on the edge of Haversham, with a whole wooded area surrounding it on three sides.

But on this bleak afternoon, with its gusting winds, overcast sky, and the smell of coming snow on the air, the place looked grim. Two of its front windows were taped where they'd been cracked, the screening on the front doors was pushed in, and the weeds, even though they were winter-dead, were littering the edges of the narrow sidewalk.

From her first impression, she would have to say that former Sheriff John Tyler was not exactly an impressive man.

She went up to the door and knocked, the sound almost lost on the wind.

Faintly, she heard the voice of a disk jockey laughing a lurid laugh, then the start of a rock'n'roll song. Abruptly, the door was thrown open, and a woman wearing nothing more than sleepiness and a man's shirt stood there.

The woman who Diane figured was about her own

age despite some severe age lines, was obviously not impressed with Sheriff Baines, either by her khaki uniform or her quiet prettiness.

"Yeah?" the woman said.

"I'm looking for John Tyler."

The woman grinned. "That's who a lot of women have been looking for. Unfortunately, there's only one place you're going to find him." From behind her back, the woman produced a fifth of cheap vodka. "Right here. That's where John Tyler lives."

The woman choked back tears that suddenly sounded in her voice, then said, "Gimme a minute, all right?"

Diane nodded, embarrassed that she had walked into the middle of what was obviously a domestic problem. She felt sorry for the woman. Not too many years ago the woman had obviously been very nice looking. It had all been ahead of her, then. Now, sadly, at least from appearances, it seemed gone from her.

When she reappeared less than two minutes later, the woman wore a white blouse, designer jeans, and a western suede jacket with long fringes. Lipstick and a touch of rouge on her cheeks had brought back a suggestion of her former beauty. Without saying a word, she walked out past Diane, carrying an overnight bag, and went down to the sidewalk to a ten-year-old Buick. She got in and drove away.

From inside, even though the winter wind was strong, Diane could smell the remnants of a misled life. Beer, vodka, stale pizza, cigarette smoke. The odors brought back her college days, when she had spent her senior year trying to overcome a failed love affair by living as wildly as she could. These were the smells she associated with bleak mornings-after.

"Mr. Tyler?"

No response.

"Mr. Tyler?"

Again, nothing.

She opened the squeaking screen door and went on inside.

She touched her fingertips to the weapon she wore on her hip. From years as a law enforcement officer, she knew that this was a classically dangerous situation.

She had no idea where Tyler was, or what his mood might be.

He could easily be holding a gun on her.

She found him then and almost smiled to herself.

John Tyler was incapable of holding a gun on anybody, at least right now.

He sat at an old-fashioned formica-topped table in the tiny kitchen, his head down on his folded arms.

Snoring.

In the next instant he startled her by jerking his head up.

She saw two things at once: a man far gone enough into booze that he had trouble focusing his eyes. And a man who at one time in his life must have possessed a real dignity. Even in these grungy circumstances, even in a wrinkled button-down white shirt and a face two days in need of a shave, John Tyler retained an air of an ironic and pensive intelligence. He wasn't handsome exactly, but there was a gravity in the brown eyes and on the wry mouth that she found very appealing.

He sat back in his chair, rubbing his face, obviously embarrassed to be found in such a state. He got a cigarette going. The smoke looked very blue when he exhaled it. In an almost boyish way, he nodded to his cigarette and said, "Supposedly, I'm going to quit these things next week." Then he said, "Supposedly, I'm going to quit a lot of things." This time his eyes fell on the empty vodka bottle in front of him. The bitterness in his voice was sharp in the small kitchen.

Once again, Diane had the sense that she was intruding in a domestic scene that was every bit as depressing as the gray day itself.

He looked at her, at her uniform, at her face, and said, "You sure look good in that uniform." He smiled with a curious melancholy. "A lot better than I ever did."

"Thank you," she said, still uneasy.

"I'm not in any trouble, am I?"

He tried to make his comment ironic, but she could hear in it the desperate, searching note of an alcoholic trying to piece together a forgotten stretch of time during which anything might have happened.

"I don't think so," she said, trying to match his ironic tone.

He threw a hand into the air. "Sorry this place is such a mess." He glanced around. "I don't know what to offer you other than a cold beer. Assuming I've got one in the refrigerator, that is."

"No thanks."

He smiled, sadly as before. "Somehow I didn't think you'd want one." He took another drag on his cigarette, exhaled, then turned his eyes on her. "So, Sheriff, what can I do for you?"

"I'd like to talk to you about a case."

He smiled. "You want my advice on a case?"

She sensed that despite his humorous way of treating the subject, he would have been flattered if that indeed had been what she wanted. "No, a case you worked on fifteen years ago. A hit-and-run involving a boy from Windhaven Orphanage."

"Oh."

The transformation was remarkable. A few moments earlier, Tyler had begun to climb out of his alcoholic shell. Now she saw his face go white and his gaze dull, as if she'd brought up something that his mind simply would not deal with. As if he'd gone into a minor form of shock.

"Windhaven," he repeated.

"Yes."

"That would be Mrs. Kilrane. And Mr. Rydell. And most especially, that would be Mr. Raymond Stockbridge himself."

He shook his head, his bitterness apparent. Then, in a very warm way, he said, "You sure you don't want that beer?"

She surprised both of them by saying, "Well, maybe I will. I was officially off duty an hour ago."

"Good," he said, "because I'd really enjoy talking to you."

The odd and unlikely thing was, Diane knew she was going to enjoy talking to him, too.

Caroline had not said anything for the past ten minutes.

She did the only thing she could do. Sit and listen. From the expression on her face, it was easy to see that she was, in equal measure, fascinated, awed, and scared by what Brian was telling her.

Occasionally, Caroline lifted one of her braided pigtails to her face and touched it idly to her lips, but other than that she was still. Perfectly still.

The two sat in one of the rooms in the basement of Windhaven, right off the main rec room with the Ping-Pong tables, the TV sets, and the Coke machines.

Then Caroline said, "Maybe you shouldn't be telling me this."

Brian was confused. "Why?"

"Because I'm scared. I really am. If you go out there again tonight and Mrs. Kilrane finds out . . ."

She cast her eyes in her lap.

Usually, thirteen-year-old Caroline regarded herself as grown up enough to handle virtually any circumstance. You got awfully self-sufficient when your parents died in a car accident when you were six years old—and when the state decided to put you in a series of orphanages rather than let you stay with an alcoholic aunt.

This was the first circumstance in several years that had really frightened her—and she wasn't sure whose future scared her most—her own or Brian's.

But Brian still pressed his point. "Listen . . . I've got to know if what happened last night—well, if it really happened. You understand that, don't you?"

Caroline had an idea. Her inquisitive blue eyes shone with it. "You really miss Davie, don't you."

Brian wondered if this was a trick question.

"Okay, so I miss Davie," he said warily. "So what?"

"Well, maybe that's why this is happening to you."

"God, you read that newspaper article about stress, too, didn't you?"

She was defensive.

"Yes, I did. So what's wrong with that? You could just be suffering from stress."

Brian nodded. In a half-whisper, he said, "Yeah, I guess. . . ."

He thought of last night. The bluish glow in the swamp. The voice calling him, needing him. *Brian . . . Help me.*

"How about meeting me near the back door at eleven o'clock?"

"Brian!" She shrieked, then clapped her hand over her mouth. She hissed, "Are you *crazy?*"

"C'mon, Caroline, you're the only friend I've got."

"But Brian—"

Just then Dodge came into view. In his white t-shirt and white trousers, his muscles bulging, his hair shining, as always, with grease, and an easy sneer tugging at his lips, he swaggered over. "I wish I had the luck you had with women, Brian," Dodge laughed.

Caroline turned pink.

Dodge leaned over, lifted one of her pigtails, and felt it. He held it, his thumb running over the silky texture. A strange, hazy look came into his eyes.

Caroline jerked away.

As she did so Dodge's hand came down hard across her mouth.

Caroline yelped.

Brian jumped to his feet and pushed both his hands, stiff-armed fashion, into Dodge's midsection.

Dodge laughed and easily tossed Brian back into the chair.

"You get a couple years older," Dodge said, looking back at Caroline, "you look me up, hear?"

Dodge left, laughing.

Caroline sat in her chair, sobbing. Brain went over and sat on the arm.

"I hate this place," she said, after her tears had subsided.

"You'll be out of here in a few weeks," Brian said.

She looked up, tears giving her eyes a silvery look. "Oh, Brian, somebody will adopt you, you'll see." She took his hand and held it fondly. "You're my best friend in the whole world."

Brian felt his usual mixture of emotions. He was glad to hear Caroline say this, but he also felt a terrible loss. In just a few weeks she would be gone from him. Forever.

"You really want me to go with you tonight, don't you?" Caroline asked.

Brian nodded.

"Then I will," she said, *"Now* can we go have some dinner? I'm starved."

8

In the fading hours of the November day, the swamp area was a viscous tarry color.

A truck driver, hurrying along the road that ran parallel to the swamp, hoping to end his day soon with a brew and some shuffleboard at a local tap, happened to glance out the window at the swamp.

This was one place the fag liberals were always bitching about.

This swamp.

Gave you hives. Gave you headaches. Gave you cancer.

Shit.

He had been driving past this swampy area ever since he'd left high school twenty years ago and not a damn thing had happened to him, even the summer he'd worked at another nearby landfill.

Hives. Headache. Cancer.

If it wasn't one thing with the fag liberals then it was another.

It was while he was thinking this that he happened to notice the glow.

Bluish, it was.

Somewhere deep within the swamp.

He was startled enough by the sight of it that he nearly ran his truck over the embankment on the right side of the road.

He stopped the truck, jumped down, went over for a look.

He hadn't brought his jacket along, so the cold wind got to him immediately.

He stood rubbing his arms, looking at the surface of the swamp that seemed to bubble despite the freezing temperature.

This was perfect hunting weather. For a moment he forgot all about the swamp and concentrated on images of hunting. Of pheasants arcing against the leaden winter sky. Of hunting dogs lathered from their searches. Of coffee pouring from a thermos like black lava. These were the things that stayed with a man, these and memories of your kids, these things and not all the political crap, or arguing with bosses or arguing with unions . . . the unchanging images of your kids at various young stages of their lives, and of hard, cold mornings when you braved the elements with your rifle and tromped through corn fields or sat in duck blinds.

Brad Stovik, the truck driver, was thinking these things when the glow began again.

At first he was too lost in his own reverie to notice the light that had brought him there in the first place.

But its effect soon got his attention.

His eyes went back to the bluish glow just about the time the first pain crackled through his head.

Instantly, Stovik put his hands viselike to his head and pushed hard, as if to compress the pain and make it go away.

But it wouldn't go away, and neither would the blood that had started pouring from his nose and mouth.

And soon from his eyes and ears, as well.

The blue glow vanished just as Stovik collapsed on the ground. His body was soaked with his own blood as he reached out a single twisted hand for help.

But there was no help.

Not anymore.

Chapter Three

1

When Brian got back to his room after his visit with Caroline and making plans for their excursion that night, he found that a strange thing had taken place.

Somebody had come into the room he had once shared with Davie Mason and removed all of Davie's things.

Every single thing. From the shirts hanging in the closet to the stack of "Jonah Hex" comic books in the corner next to the bureau.

Gone.

Brian checked through everything just to be sure that his impression was correct. It was. Somebody had literally taken everything. As if they wanted all memory of Davie to vanish. Entirely.

He remembered the place under Davie's bed where his friend had stashed things—special things like

Indian head nickels, a ticket stub from a Billy Joel concert and, once, a marijuana cigarette that he'd gotten from a kid in the city—Davie's very special hiding place.

Had they discovered that, too?

Brian went over to Davie's bed and got down on his knees. He pushed his hand up under the mattress, to a tear in the fabric where Davie had stuffed his loot.

At first he felt nothing.

So they *had* found the hiding place, he thought glumly, feeling that their intrusion had somehow violated Davie's memory.

Then his fingers contacted something metallic and sharp. Sharp enough to puncture his finger.

Cursing, he withdrew his hand, sucked on the finger until he drew a tiny droplet of blood that left a steely tang in his mouth.

More cautiously, he put his hand back up under the mattress, felt around very, very slowly, and once again made contact with the metal thing.

It took two full minutes to pull the thing from the mattress stuffing where Davie had secreted the metal object.

What he finally held in his hands, what his eyes fell upon, he could scarcely believe.

There in the palm of his hand lay a tin soldier, identical to the one that Mr. Stockbridge had given Brian earlier in the day.

2

Sheriff Diane Baines had been more than happy to agree to have dinner with John Tyler. Anything to escape his depressing little house and sit in clean surroundings without the stench of cigarette smoke and stale beer.

The diner was busy with dinnertime. Workers from a nearby factory ate meals prepared earlier and kept in steam tables.

Diane liked the smell of cooked roast beef and vegetables. She also liked the hearty way the men ate and laughed. From a blue-collar family herself, she had always suspected that the virtues that had made the country great began to wane as fewer and fewer people worked with their hands.

At first her uniform fascinated most of the men who sat around the booth that she and Tyler occupied. But gradually the men went back to their food, beginning to watch the clock. Dinner break would soon be over.

Thus far Diane had learned these things about Tyler: He was a divorced man in his mid-forties who had gotten into law enforcement after a two-hitch term in the Navy back in the early 1960s. Presently, he worked thirty hours a week as a security guard. If he had worked full time, he had noted ruefully, they would have had to offer him health insurance.

Tyler had offered all this information without any resentment at all. Obviously, Diane's questions had meant to probe, and he seemed to understand this and acknowledge that as sheriff, it was her right to ask.

Only when she'd raised the subject of the hit-and-run accident fifteen years earlier had the cloudiness come over his eyes, had his words become evasive. It was shortly after, her question left unanswered, that he'd suggested that they go out to the diner. Obviously it had seemed to him a good way of quietly dropping the subject of the car accident.

Diane, who considered two pounds above her normal weight to be a severe crime against nature, ordered a slice of beef, a single slice of wheat toast, and a small salad.

When she looked up from her menu, she saw that Tyler was watching her with some amusement.

"What's so funny?" she said good-naturedly.

He shrugged. "The people who watch their weight generally don't need to. Fat people eat what they want."

For a time that was all he said. He ordered the full dinner. Then he excused himself and went to the men's room. As he walked to the back, she saw a few of the men nod toward him and exchange whispers and smirks. She'd heard stories about Tyler from time to time. He was now considered a strange man, and worse, an alcoholic. Thus far she would have had to agree with both estimations of the man. Still, she felt sorry for him.

Diane spent her few minutes alone looking through her pocket-size notebook where she kept her

"To Do" list. No wonder she hadn't met a new man yet. There was literally no time. There would be less time when the election drew nearer.

He came back and sat down. "Guess I just needed a few minutes alone."

She studied his face, trying to figure out what he was talking about. Hadn't he just gone to the john?

"I went outside and had a smoke," he said, as if reading her mind.

"Oh, I see," Diane said. But she didn't see at all. He was a strange man, indeed.

"The hit-and-run you mentioned. I had to kind of work myself up to talking about it."

Before he could continue, their food came.

The next few minutes, they spent their time enjoying their food.

But she was too much the law officer to let his silence alone. She said, "The hit-and-run must've really upset you."

"It's why I quit my job as sheriff."

She paused over a bite of her salad. "You quit? I thought your term expired."

His smile was not without melancholy. "Some of the rumors about me are true. Some aren't. Rumor number one, that the voters would have tossed me out—not true. Actually, I was a very popular sheriff. Rumor number two, that I had a drinking problem when I was sheriff—not true." He flushed and his eyes fell to the hand he had wound around a glass of beer. "That didn't come till later."

She laughed. Gently. "So just which rumors *are* true?"

He got serious suddenly. "The one about me

hating the Stockbridge family and the way they run this town." He shook his head. "By the time I quit, I didn't have much self-respect left. I mean, I know you have to kowtow to a certain number of people in any kind of job, but the situation with the Stockbridge family was unbelievable. If one of their in-laws got so much as a parking ticket, Raymond Stockbridge or one of his close family members would be on the phone chewing me out. They absolutely wouldn't let me do my job as sheriff. And I assume things haven't changed much."

"Unfortunately, they haven't." She tried to keep the bitterness from her voice, but it wasn't easy. During her time in Haversham she had come to see the Stockbridge family as being as criminal in their way as any bank robber or murderer. The liberties they took with the law were unbelievable.

"Think of what it would be like to be police chief," he said.

She smiled. Agreed. "Impossible."

"Maybe that's why they've all been such flunkies."

As county sheriff, Diane had to endure innumerable indignities, but not nearly as many as the police chief of Haversham. Since most of the Stockbridges lived in town, it was the chief who bore the brunt of their whining, cheating, and threats. For that reason, the good officers came and went with alarming rapidity, while only the yes-men and the flunkies stayed. That was Diane's fear—that even playing along to the extent she had with the Stockbridges had compromised her in subtle yet profound ways that she could not yet understand.

"I think they had something to do with it."

Diane, who had been lost in her own thoughts, looked up and said, "What?"

"I think they had something to do with it. The Stockbridges. With the hit-and-run. But I couldn't prove it, so that's why I quit."

Now that he'd said it, Diane realized why he had been so reluctant to bring up the subject. In Haversham, to make such an accusation was a good way to get yourself into very serious trouble.

She was just about to speak when the beeper she carried on her belt ignited.

The men in the restaurant reacted as if a hand grenade had been thrown in their midst. Jerking around. Startled.

"Excuse me," she said.

She found a pay phone in the back and dialed her office immediately.

Deputy Bill Farnsworth was on the other end of the receiver. "Strange one," he said. "At least that's what Doc Adams tells me. Truck driver. Blood all over the place."

"I'm not sure what that means, Bill."

He laughed uneasily. "Neither is Doc Adams. Says he's never seen anything like it."

"Where's Adams now?"

"City General. Doing an autopsy."

"I'll be there in ten minutes."

He paused. "Did you, uh, find Tyler?"

"Yes, I did."

Again the pause. What was wrong with him? "What'd you think?"

"Aside from an obvious drinking problem, he seems nice."

This time the deputy's voice was very tight. "Maybe I should be jealous. The sheriff always had a lot of women around him. I don't want one of them to be you."

Diane thought of the faded beauty who had been leaving Tyler's when she'd arrived. Yes, now that Bill mentioned it, Tyler did seem to be one of those men certain types of women would gravitate to. Women who liked to care for wounded animals. She was enough like that herself to recognize the impulse.

"I don't think you've got anything to worry about," Diane said. But even as she spoke she thought of how oddly relaxed Tyler made her feel. She hadn't felt like that around a man in a long time. "I'll be at City General in ten minutes," she said, and hung up.

At the table, Tyler had ordered a beer. Curiously, he hadn't touched it. He just sat staring at it, as if debating with himself whether or not to drink it. Diane found herself hoping the answer would be no.

Diane didn't have time to sit down. "Something's come up. Do you suppose you could find a ride home?"

He looked up and the hurt was clear in his eyes. "You have to go?"

"I'm afraid I do."

He smiled gently. "Hell, I was just beginning to enjoy myself."

She let herself say what she felt. "So was I." Then she turned to go.

"You can always call me," he said.

She grinned. "And you can always call me, too." Then she left.

3

Just after dinner it started to rain again.

Brian lay on his bed in the darkness. The only light was the illumination from the streetlight through the north window.

The shadowy light fell on the two tin soldiers before him on the bed.

One of the soldiers was his. The other had belonged to Davie Mason.

But why hadn't Davie told him about the soldier? His friend had told him about everything else—that was the whole basis of their friendship, the fact that they weren't afraid to discuss anything with each other—but for some reason Davie had kept the soldier from Brian.

Why?

Tired from too much food, Brian lay on his back and stared at the ceiling.

He needed to rest, but he had to be careful not to go to sleep. Less than three hours from now he and Caroline would be going to the swamp.

To find out the truth.

His thoughts turned back to the soldier and Mr. Stockbridge. Six hours of the forty-eight the ominous man had given him were already gone.

Brian couldn't even imagine what the punishment would be like.

He trembled.

Maybe it would have been better just to tell him the truth.

That he'd gone out to the swamp.

That he'd imagined that his friend Davie Mason had called to him.

Yes, that was it. Mr. Stockbridge would have pointed out that things like dead friends calling people just didn't happen. He probably would have felt sorry for Brian, and the matter would have been closed, with no threats about forty-eight hours or anything like that.

Brian was almost tempted to go downstairs and find Mrs. Kilrane and ask her to call her father. Then Brian would tell him what had happened—or what he had imagined had happened—and then they all would have a big laugh. Including Mrs. Kilrane. Yes, even Mrs. Kilrane would find the humor in this particular situation and laugh right along with them.

Brian

He had been falling asleep lying there on the bed thinking about how nice it would be to hear Mrs. Kilrane laugh, and then something had startled him back from the brink of sleep.

Brian

Tonight there was an urgent edge to the voice. As if it were summoning him this very moment to the swamp.

Brian

He sat up in bed and pressed his hands hard over his ears in an attempt to stop the voice from entering his hearing.

But there was no stopping it.

The voice remained, compelling, tireless, spooky.

He jumped up from the bed and ran out into the hall.

Two boys were having a pillow fight, one smashing the other and then standing still to take his own turn at getting hit.

Brian guessed his face looked pretty strange because both boys stopped, stared at him then looked at each other.

Brian, embarrassed, rushed back into his room and threw himself on his bed.

Once again he covered his ears, but it did no good.

Brian

The voice remained.

He had wanted to ask the boys in the hall if they, too, heard the voice. But he knew better. Knew somehow that only he could hear it. Asking them would only enhance his reputation for being strange.

Then the voice died, like an echo disappearing in the vast distances between mountain peaks, and gave Brian rest.

He even dozed off for a time. No voice disturbed him.

When he awoke the hallway was quiet. It was past lights-out time.

No voice.

Brian felt as if he were finally waking from a nightmare that had lasted nearly twenty-four hours.

There was no sense in his and Caroline's going to the swamp tonight. He had simply imagined Davie's voice. He would tell that to Mr. Stockbridge and everything would be better again.

He had gotten up to take off his clothes for the night when he made the mistake of glancing out the south window.

At the swamp.

Where the blue glow seemed to beckon to him.

Brian

No doubt now where the voice had come from. No doubt at all.

Chapter Four

1

Diane had never forgotten her first experience in a morgue. It was one that her duties as sheriff forced her to relive again and again. . . .

This was ten years ago, back on the West Coast when she'd just been starting out as a cop. After six months on the beat she'd assumed she'd seen everything, every type of human abuse, excess, and perversion. She'd assumed she couldn't be shocked.

Then one night she accompanied a detective to the big city morgue.

And almost lost her religious faith.

Seeing human bodies stockpiled inside drawers that pull out and push in on casters took something away from the concept of God.

Seeing human bodies with big holes in them where certain of their innards had been pulled out for autopsies—

Or seeing human bodies with numbered tags on their toes like so much merchandise—

Diane had never forgotten any of these things, including the acrid smell, and the numbing coldness of the place, and the casual, almost profane way the morgue workers conducted themselves—as if they weren't at all impressed with the enormity of the spectacle around them.

Tonight Diane felt some of the same things as she stood outside the glass doors leading to the morgue in the basement of City General.

Here the morgue didn't sprawl for half a floor, as it did in the city. It was simply a large, tan-tiled room with cubicles for offices at the west end and a bank of body drawers at the east.

Peering through the door, not quite up to opening it yet, Diane saw Doc Adams sitting on the edge of the reception desk talking to Mavis Farley. Doc Adams was a scruffy man in his mid-fifties, one given to polyester suits that nonetheless looked wrinkled, Hush Puppy shoes, a pipe that hadn't been cleaned in probably decades, and a flamboyantly flirtatious style with ladies of any age. Even now he was laughing along with Mavis Farley, the morgue's nightshift person. Mavis was a fleshy woman whose misuse of makeup gave her cheeky face a doll-like aspect. She was in her late forties and the obviously proud possessor of a huge pair of breasts, which Doc Adams kept taking enthusiastic and quite public glances at as they talked.

When Diane came through the door, they looked up like guilty children.

"Sorry for interrupting your dinner," Adams said, hopping down from Mavis' desk. He jammed his pipe in his mouth and drew his body to its full five-feet-five-inch height.

"How are you, Sheriff?" Mavis said warmly. The woman was, in her way, a feminist. She thought it was wonderful that the county had a female sheriff.

At least until next election.

Mavis had already offered several times to work in Diane's campaign.

"A little tired, I guess," Diane said. The pace of the last few days were starting to take their toll. The death of David Mason at Windhaven Orphanage had cost her her peace of mind from the first moment she'd heard about it.

Something was wrong out there.

"How about a cup of coffee?" Mavis said.

"Great. I'd really appreciate it."

When Mavis went over to the Mr. Coffee, Doc Adams took the pipe out of his mouth and shook his head. "Don't exactly know what to tell you."

"About the man who was brought in?"

Doc Adams nodded. "Never seen anything quite like it." He smiled with tender eyes. "In my med school days I always heard about it, but I never quite believed it."

Mavis was back with the coffee.

Diane thanked her, sipped at the steaming liquid.

"You ready to go in?" Doc Adams asked.

"Would it do any good if I said no?" Diane smiled.

"Nope."

"Well, let's go, then."

At the opposite end of the big room, where the fluorescent light seemed even harsher, Doc Adams paused before a bank of huge drawers. He put his hand on one of them, tapped it.

"In college, I always heard about the rare person who died from spontaneous combustion."

"Somebody who literally explodes?"

"Exactly."

"And that's what we're dealing with here?"

He looked at her evenly. "To be honest, Diane, I'm not sure what we're dealing with."

He pulled open the drawer.

Diane's dread of morgues was instantly realized.

The thing that lay before her had once been a man, but his remains gave only a vague indication of that fact.

Parts of Brad Stovik's flesh appeared to have been burned, charred black. Other parts looked as if the flesh had burst outward in huge open wounds. His nose had been ripped away and one of his hands was a bloody stump.

Doc Adams closed the drawer.

"Sorry," he said. "But I had to show you so you'd know what I was talking about."

Diane nodded, knowing that she probably looked pale and strained.

"I understand," she said.

"Believe me," Doc Adams said. "That my was first reaction, too." He thumped his stomach. "Damn near lost my cookies."

He led them back to the cubicle he used when he worked at the morgue. Otherwise she always saw him

76

in his ranch house, which doubled as his general practitioner office, as well.

"So you don't have any idea what happened?"

"Not a clue so far," Doc Adams said. "You want some more coffee?"

Diane shook her head.

"I've spent the last two hours going through my medical books," Doc Adams went on, "but I just can't find a reasonable explanation."

"Not even spontaneous combustion?"

"Not the way the books describe it. I mean, there are definitely certain similarities, but this is more— the burning, for instance. Third-degree burns over large patches of his body. That hasn't been found on victims of spontaneous combustion in the past."

"So where does that leave us?"

"Nowhere, as far as I can see." He paused. For all his homespun ways, Doc Adams enjoyed being dramatic every once in a while. "Unless you give a little bit of credence to my theory."

Diane smiled. "I always give credence to your theories, Doc. Even when they're wrong."

He laughed. "Well, if you'll have another cup of coffee with me, I'll tell you all about it." His blue eyes glittered. "Sneaky way to get a pretty lady to spend some time with me."

"Very sneaky."

He started off toward the Mr. Coffee.

Diane said, "Aren't you even going to give me a hint?"

"About my theory?"

"Ummm-hmmm."

He was serious suddenly. "It's probably the kind of thing nobody is going to want to hear about."

"Try me."

Doc Adams frowned. "Well, Diane, I think there's at least a possibility that Brad Stovik's death had to do with that chemical dump next to Windhaven Orphanage."

2

"That wasn't very smart," Mrs. Kilrane said. "In fact, it was very stupid."

"It's just a toy, a harmless toy."

"A harmless toy."

The derision in Mrs. Kilrane's voice seemed to cool even the ardor of the fire that burned and snapped behind the grate.

The Stockbridge den looked big enough to house the Library of congress. Twenty-foot built-in bookcases filled with leather-bound editions soared to the shadows at ceiling level. A fire in a fireplace the size of a small camper roared at one end of the room, where Mrs. Kilrane and her father sat. In the dancing firelight could be seen glimpses of original art by Renoir, Picasso, Grant Wood. Good investments, all.

Mrs. Kilrane paced.

That was her way in times of anxiety.

Hands behind her back, moving back and forth with military precision, a riding crop dangling from her heavy hands, she walked off her frustrations.

Or tried to.

She looked at the man before her. Her lip turned upward in a kind of sneer.

Raymond Stockbridge.

The most feared man in the entire county.

She brought her riding crop down on the long

conference table. The sound it made forced Stock-bridge to rear up in his chair. No easy feat for a man of his bulk.

"I've told you never to hand out those toy soldiers again. You disobeyed me—just like you used to disobey Mother." Behind the firelight dancing on the surfaces of her glasses, her dark eyes narrowed. "You know what's going to happen, don't you?"

"Please, Lavonne. Please."

The riding crop came down again. "I told you never to call me that!"

"Lavonne" sounded like a little girl. She much preferred the authoritative sound of "Mrs. Kilrane," the name bequeathed her by her late husband.

"Please," he pleaded again.

The most powerful man in the county.

Her lip curled upward again.

"You're going upstairs. To the attic."

"No, please, please."

But obviously he knew it was no use.

"You don't know what it's like up there," Stockbridge said. "It scares me."

"That's just what you need, Father. To be scared. So you're never foolish enough to hand out toy soldiers again. Do you understand?"

She hovered over him, her riding crop angled like a weapon. "Now come on. Lift your fat carcass out of that chair and get upstairs to the attic."

3

Brian stood at the top of the stairs. In his ears, his breathing sounded loud as drums. He was sure others could hear it, too.

Sweat chilled him beneath his slicker.

At this late hour the orphanage was a place of deep shadow and queer noises.

He put one foot down on the carpeted step. Then the next foot.

He started downward, into the pitch blackness of the place.

The sound he heard next slammed him back against the wall.

Somewhere on the second floor a door had opened. And the sound of a terrible singer could be heard on a scratchy old record.

Judy Garland.

Mr. Rydell was playing his Judy Garland records again.

From the shadows Brian watched, his heart still pounding from the sudden intrusion of noise, as Mr. Rydell made his way down the hallway to the bathroom. Mr. Rydell was swathed in a silk robe and carried his toothbrush and Colgate tube with almost religious reverence.

Mr. Rydell was getting ready for a good night's sleep, as he always liked to call it.

Brian decided to move.

No sense wasting any more time.

He started down the stairs.

Caroline couldn't believe it.

Mr. Rydell appeared out of the gloom in the hallway like an apparition.

"Hello, Mr. Rydell."

She tried to make it sound as if they were passing each other on a fine spring morning, merely exchanging pleasant hellos.

But, of course, Mr. Rydell knew better.

His eyes fell on her, on the sweater and jeans and boots she wore, on the scarf wound round her neck, on the heavy winter coat she had been shrugging into.

"And just where do you think you're going, young lady?" Mr. Rydell said in his tartest voice.

All Caroline could think of was how she was going to let Brian down.

As an orphan, she knew what it meant to be let down, to have people constantly break their word.

Ordinarily, being what folks like to call "a good little girl," Caroline would have given in to the tone of Mr. Rydell's voice.

Ordinarily.

But not tonight.

Brian needed help, and by God she was going to help him.

One way or the other.

"I must have been sleepwalking," she said.

"Sleepwalking?"

"Yes. I do that, you know."

"No, I didn't know."

"Sure. All the time."

"Why haven't I ever run across any reference to it in your file? Why hasn't Mrs. Kilrane ever mentioned it?"

Caroline frowned. "It's true, Mr. Rydell. I put on my clothes and wander all over the place. I'm not even aware of it until somebody wakes me up."

"You just woke up now?" he asked, still sounding very suspicious.

"Just when I heard you coming down the hall. You can imagine how embarrassed I was."

"So now you're going back to bed?"

"Straight back to bed, Mr. Rydell."

He was going to give it one last try. "I've never heard of anybody who puts on clothes to sleepwalk."

"That's very common, Mr. Rydell."

He gave her a stern look. He had always struck her as, in equal parts, funny and sad. Now he seemed just plain funny, his twitchy little mustache and hip-cocked stance making his tart mannerisms a bit comic. "How do you know so much about sleep-walking?"

"I spend most of my time reading about it."

What a good liar she was becoming. She was so good at it, she frightened herself. What if, by the time she was fourteen, say, she started *liking* lying? Caroline spent a good deal of her time worrying about things like that.

"I thought you spent most of your time reading Judy Blume."

"Between Judy Blume books, I mean. That's when

I read about sleepwalking."

Still Mr. Rydell looked skeptical. But he also looked impatient with the conversation. "We'll talk about this in the morning."

"Yes, Mr. Rydell."

"Straight back to bed, now."

"Yes, Mr. Rydell."

"And no reading. Straight to sleep."

"Yes, Mr. Rydell."

"Good night."

"Good night."

With that, Mr. Rydell preceded her down the hall, pausing at her room to make sure she went inside and closed the door.

Which she did, of course.

Having no choice.

Where was she?

By now Brian stood next to the back door, the one with the flap for dogs, which he'd learned to shimmy through, listening to the sounds of the orphanage as the time pushed on to midnight.

The grandfather clock.

The steady thrumming of the refrigerator motor.

The creaks and groans of innumerable corners and crevices and hollows.

Where was she?

The back porch where he stood overlooked a farm field. Frost covered the fallen corn stalks, sheening in the moonlight. Naked trees were silhouetted against the round yellow disk of moon. A single dog barked at the night.

Where was she?

Caroline waited till she heard the water running down the hall.

That would be Mr. Rydell.

She put her hand on the doorknob.

Eased it rightward with a single gloved hand.

And then the light came on.

She whirled around as if she'd been shot.

Gwen, her chunky roommate, spoke in what seemed to be a foreign language. Actually, she was still mostly asleep and mumbling. Of course, she mumbled when she was awake, too.

"What?" Caroline whispered, unable to figure out what Gwen was saying.

Gwen looked peeved. "I said, Where are you going?"

There wasn't time to lie. "Out."

"Out?"

"Yes. And don't talk so loudly."

"Do you know what'll happen if weird Mr. Rydell catches you?"

"He already has."

"What?"

Caroline explained.

"God, you're really asking for it, Caroline. It's a good thing you're leaving in two weeks," Gwen said, referring to Caroline's impending adoption.

Caroline moved back to the door. "Turn out the light, okay, Gwen?"

"You going to tell me where you're going?"

"No."

"Shit, c'mon, Caroline."

"Maybe I'll tell you later."

"Promise?"

"Promise." Caroline wondered to herself if she were lying again.

The light went out.

Caroline wished Gwen wasn't breathing so hard in the darkness.

Made it difficult to hear.

But from what her ears told her, now was as good a time as any to make her break.

"Bye," she whispered.

And was gone.

She wasn't coming.

Brian felt angry and foolish.

No matter how many times he told himself never to count on people keeping their word, he still trusted them. . . .

And was constantly disappointed for his troubles.

"Hi."

He had been looking out the back window, at the frosty landscape and the single lonely dog moving in wide circles around the chemical site, when he heard the word whispered in the apple-smelling darkness of the back porch.

It was as if God himself had reached down and touched Brian on the shoulder.

"You ready?" she asked.

86

He could never recall being happier than at this moment.

"You ready?" she asked again.

"Yeah," he said.

"You scared?"

"Huh-uh," he said.

"I am."

He smiled. "Yeah, so am I."

4

There was no rain tonight, but there was a wind that numbed the bones and worked like an anesthetic on the flesh.

Brian grabbed Caroline's hand as they pressed against the wall of wind, the trees whipping naked limbs about them, snow spitting at their eyes.

A fog had rolled in from the nearby river, wraiths of silver dispersing like smoke over the surface of the chemical site.

At the fence Caroline paused, as if they had come to an insurmountable obstacle in their journey.

"I'm wearing my best jeans," she said, half hollering about the wailing wind.

"What?" Brian said, unable to hear her.

"My jeans," she said, pointing to them.

"What about your jeans?"

"They're my *best* ones!"

Brian misunderstood. "Yeah, they're really nice."

She grabbed him, pulled him nearer. "No, you don't understand. They're my best jeans. I'm afraid of tearing them on the fence here."

"Oh," Brian said.

What he did next surprised both of them.

He'd seen it a hundred times in the old movies on afternoon television.

How the brave hero picks up the heroine as if

they're about to enter their wedding suite and helps her across the threshold.

"Brian!" she giggled.

Their mood of tension from sneaking out was banished now, at least for the moment.

Brian had not felt this kind of freedom for a long time. Even with his nose frozen numb, his eyes watering from the chill, and his fingers stiff as sticks. He hefted her up in his arms and started for the fenced-off area before them, the area that now resembled a World War I battlefield in its barrenness and desolation.

Right up to the fence their festive mood continued to cut against the night.

Then it vanished instantly and utterly with the appearance of the blue glow that cast its light against the drifting fog directly overhead.

"God," she said, "what's that?"

"Just what I told you about."

"God."

"Yeah."

Gently, she slid from his arms, found purchase on the frozen mud surrounding the chemical site.

"What is it?"

"I don't know," Brian said.

For long moments the wind had subsided, so they could hear each other speak.

Now it rose again, wailing, pushing them closer to the barbed wire of the fence, to the eerie blue glow emanating from the turgid puddle of chemicals before them.

"Come on," Brian said.

But already his voice was lost again.

He put a gloved hand on one strand of wire and held it up to permit himself passage through. When he was on the other side, he held the fencing apart so Caroline could come through, too."

Two minutes later they stood on the lip of the pool itself.

There was no sign of the glow.

"Do you hear anything?" Caroline shouted at Brian. "Any voices in your head?"

"No."

"You sure?"

"I'm sure."

They were yelling again.

"Concentrate," she said.

"Okay."

Brian closed his eyes.

The wind nearly knocked him over.

She caught him.

He wanted to throw his arms around her. Kiss her. He knew he should be concentrating, like she'd told him, but he couldn't help himself.

She pushed him, playfully.

"Come on, Brian, this is serious."

"I know."

"Then come *on*."

Whenever she started emphasizing words, he knew she was serious.

He went back to standing like a wooden Indian in the wind.

Eyes closed.

Concentrating.

A few times he thought he heard the stirrings of a voice in his head . . . but no, nothing.

"You hear anything?"

"Not yet."

"Maybe he doesn't want to talk because I'm here."

Actually, Brian had thought of that.

Maybe Davie Mason wanted to keep his conversations with Brian strictly private.

"Nah, Davie always liked you."

"Yeah, but maybe he has different opinions now that he's dead."

"I don't think so."

"He likes the same stuff?"

"I suppose. Yeah." Brian tried to sound definitive about his answer.

"Do dead people watch the Cubs?" she asked.

"When he contacts me again, I'll ask him."

Brian was pleased with the way this night had turned out. Except for the strange blue glow, which might be explainable given the nature of the chemical dump itself, nothing supernatural had happened. Which meant that he might very well have been imagining things. Which meant, finally, that everything would go back to its normal self.

"Look!" Caroline shouted, pointing.

This time the blue glow widened and deepened in its color.

And this time the voice filling Brian's brain was unmistakable.

Brian, help me.

Brian clamped his hands to his head. The voice was so loud. Too loud.

Something else was happening to him, too, though Brian wasn't quite sure what.

A strange feeling pulsing through his body, as if a

91

new kind of highly charged blood had been inserted in his veins.

He felt a raw strength in his arms and hands and legs that he'd never known before.

Caroline began to scream.

He turned to her to see what was the matter, but her screams only grew louder. She threw her hands over her face, as if to protect herself.

For a moment he didn't realize the significance of what she was doing.

But as he moved toward her, he began to understand that what was frightening her was not the night, not the chemical site, but himself.

She was trying to escape from *him*.

He tried to say some reassuring words, but as his mouth opened and his tongue began to form a syllable, he realized that he could not talk.

His skin crawled with the strength he felt. Then he saw that the hot stretches of skin on his hands appeared—*blue*.

He stared in dumb disbelief at his hands.

They glowed with the same color as the chemical site. The voice pounded again and again in his brain, summoning him.

He reached out a hand for her to take.

She had backed up to the barbed wire, was trying to climb through the fencing.

He saw her jacket collar get caught on a barb.

She was trapped.

She sank to the ground.

Her hands went up in a pleading gesture as he moved toward her.

The acrid smell of the dump and the cold, clear

smell of what was now spitting snow contrasted sharply with each other—only feeding Brian's sense of disorientation.

"Help me," he cried to Caroline.

But his voice was slowed down grotesquely, like a forty-five rpm record played at thirty-three.

"Help me," he said again.

But again the effect was the same.

He felt rage and frustration and went stumbling away from her, knowing that she was too afraid to help him. A powerful headache seized him then, one blinding in its fury. He seemed to "see" without quite being able to focus.

He went to the edge of the dump and looked at the coarse chemical surface before him. By now the headache was like two metal bands being squeezed tighter and tighter across his skull.

Dimly he became aware of the pulsing blue light in the swamp—its rhythms keyed somehow to the rhythms of his headache.

The blue glow was communicating with him— no, instructing him.

Pressing his hands to his head, he turned back toward Caroline, just in time to see her scramble back toward the fencing to freedom.

He did not want her to go.

That was all he knew at that instant—that he had never felt lonelier or more isolated—and that he needed Caroline with him.

In the bitter night his eyes raised to the tree that stood above her, and the headache became even worse. He felt his body tremble as if he were about to fly apart—and then he saw branches on the tree ignite and begin to break off and fall in flames to the ground.

It took him a full minute to realize that the branch had been severed because he had willed it to be severed.

Pain seared through his skull, and he fell to the cold, hard ground, unconscious.

At first she tried holding him and rocking him as she might have a baby. Next she tried standing him up and walking him around. Both efforts were useless. He seemed to be in some kind of trance, and she was afraid she knew its source—Davie Mason.

Caroline stood in the bitter wind and looked at the dump site. The blue glow had faded, but not her sense that just below its churning waters was a force more destructive and terrible than anything she'd ever imagined.

And Brian, her very best friend, was in its grasp.

Chapter Five

1

During the worst of her heartbreak, Diane had done several strange and embarrassing things, not the least of which was to buy a pair of cotton pullover pajamas with feet in them. She always referred to them as her "bunny jammies." She supposed that it was a way of dealing with the fact that her husband had dumped her—reverting to certain emblems of her childhood when her mother and father had been there to protect her.

None of the men she slept with from time to time ever found her bunny jammies very funny.

She wasn't sure if this was her fault for being silly or theirs for having no sense of humor.

She wore the jammies now, sitting Indian-legged in front of the TV, watching a John Payne and Sonja Henie ice skating romance on the tube.

In front of her was a green Tupperware bowl filled

with popcorn that glistened with safflower oil and salt. A Diet Coke, sweating from ice, sat nearby.

Pig-out food.

She was no drinker, so this was the only way she could cope with the events of tonight.

The disquieting time she'd had with the ex-sheriff John Tyler—what did she find so charming about him?

And then being at the morgue with the man who'd exploded.

Yes, definitely, it was a night for bunny jammies and small-scale pigging out (if she'd been major-scale pigging out, she would have taken the Sarah Lee cheesecake from the freezer and really done things up right).

She leaned back against the threadbare couch and enjoyed herself for the next ten minutes, the lovely images of Sonja and John Payne flickering through the darkness, the popcorn warm and salty, the Coke just the right temperature.

The wind, like a childhood monster, pressed and rattled at the window, but she didn't care, feeling snug inside.

Then the phone rang.

And she said something that would never have issued from the lips of Sonja Henie. She rose up and said, "Now who the hell could that be?"

It was like junior high school and the time he'd called Cindy Traynor.

Asking her to go tandem bike riding with him.

He literally thought he'd have a heart attack while

96

the phone rang.

He'd been terrified, unable to decide which fate would be worse—if she didn't answer, or if she did.

Here he was, at his age, still scared.

Tyler knew he was calling Diane Baines with information that could wait till tomorrow.

He'd gotten a call from Gus Fenster, who'd worked at the orphanage the day Davie Mason had died.

Mrs. Kilrane, the paper said, claimed that Fenster, a local free-lance carpenter, was at least partly to blame for the boy's death because Fenster hadn't fixed a step leading to the basement—the step Davie had tripped on as he'd tumbled to his death.

Earlier tonight Fenster had called Tyler, saying that there had been nothing wrong with the step—that it had been "doctored" after the fall to look in disrepair.

Fenster's implication was clear.

Davie Mason had been murdered.

Fenster had called Tyler the way many people did. Even given the former sheriff's excessive fondness for the bottle, the locals felt they could trust him. Those locals, at any rate, who did not trust anybody on the payroll of the Stockbridge family, which included Sheriff Diane Baines.

So now he had a reason to call her. However slight. And he was taking advantage of it.

"Hello."

The irritation in her voice was obvious.

He wondered suddenly if she might have a lover with her. If—

"Hello," he said, shyness reducing his voice almost to a whisper. "This is John Tyler."

97

Then she startled him.

Her tone changed abruptly and she said, "Why, hello."

"I'm sorry I'm calling so late."

"It's not that late. Eleven-thirty or so."

"Were you asleep."

"Pigging out, actually."

"That's hard to imagine. You can't weigh much more than a hundred-ten or so."

She laughed. "I'm going to send you the car of your choice for being such a good liar."

He paused. Still nervous. "You're sure I'm not interrupting?"

"Not at all." Then, "Do you like Sonja Henie?"

"The ice skater?"

"Yes."

"Well, when I was fourteen or so her movies used to be on TV all the time, and I guess I sort of had a crush on her. Boy, I haven't thought about her in a long time."

"Do you like popcorn?"

"Love it."

At the mention of popcorn, his stomach tightened. Meeting her tonight had affected him in a strange way—he'd passed up his nightly quota of beer, and food, as well. Instead, he'd started smoking Winstons with teenage intensity.

"That sounds good, actually. Popcorn."

"How would you like to share a bowl with me?"

"Are you serious?"

"Sure."

"That'd be great."

He didn't even try to keep the pleasure out of his voice.

"You're sure it wouldn't be an imposition?"

"Not at all. I'd like the company."

"Well, great."

"Just give me twenty minutes or so to get out of my bunny jammies."

He laughed. "You mean literally with a tail?"

"No tail, but feet—they've got feet."

He laughed again. "You'd better not let the voters know about those. Your opponent could make a great case for you being unfit."

She laughed, too. "That's one of my secret dreads."

He knew he was going to have to spoil the mood of their conversation. "When I get there, I'm going to have to talk a little business."

"Serious business?"

"Yes," he said, "very serious."

2

"It really happened, didn't it?"

There was a panel truck parked behind the orphanage. Brian and Caroline had climbed in the back of it to get away from the wind and the cold.

For a time neither said anything.

Their clothes smelled of the night, the truck of oil. The only light was in the two small windows in the back door. Streetlight shadowed by tree limbs. In the front the seats smelled like leather. The wind came up. The truck rocked.

Brian's eyes were closed. He felt as if he were on a raft in the middle of an endless ocean.

Drifting.

He felt Caroline's knee pressed against his arm. In the entire vast universe, her touch was the only comfort.

His memory of what had happened earlier was like a fever dream.

"Did he speak to you?"

"Davie?" Brian asked. He kept his eyes closed.

"Umm-hmm."

"Sort of."

"What did he say?"

For a time Brian said nothing, simply listened to the wind rock the truck.

"What did he say?" Caroline persisted.

"He didn't just die. He was killed. Just like the others."

"What others?"

"I'm not sure."

"He didn't explain?"

"No."

She sank back against the interior wall, her knee falling away from him.

"I wish we could go away," she said, snuggling into his arm.

"So do I."

"To Hawaii. I saw some slides of it the other day. It was beautiful."

"Yeah, Hawaii," he said.

But then the wind came up again, and Hawaii might as well have been on the other side of the galaxy.

A jagged piece of dim light fell on his hand, on the fingers of it. Had it only been a trick of the light before that had made it look blue?

His eyes rose and held in the direction of the swampy area.

He knew with a certainty that oppressed him like a physical weight that something terrible had been set in motion—something he had no control over whatsoever.

3

You could hear it in the woman's voice.

Passion.

Gus Fenster expected her to start breathing heavy at any time now.

Just like they did in the porno movies he sometimes snuck into.

As a sixty-two-year-old man who'd been three times married and three times divorced, Gus had no romantic interest in women these days—only sexual.

He wasn't sure whose fault this was. He had been faithful to each of his wives (though two of them had been anything but faithful to him) and he had joyfully honored every brithday, anniversary, and holiday important to them. He had brought them every dime he earned as a self-employed carpenter and had gone with them to every church, honkytonk, and shopping center they requested. If they had had an argument, he had invariably taken the blame, and if they were happy he had credited it all to them.

But they had left him.

One took a taxi.

Another took a moving van.

And the third had left on the back end of a big Harley, her man, named Pig Iron, straddled across the front of the fearsome machine.

He was never sure why.

Over one of them he had cried; over another he had smashed his hand in three places; and over the last one he had spent three days inside a whorehouse, without once even so much looking outside. It was like being aboard a submarine at the bottom of the ocean. Day merged into night, one woman became interchangeable with another, breakfast began to taste like dinner. By the time he left there his prostate felt as if it had been cleaned out with surgical instruments.

Not that any of this made him wiser. He still had no idea why they'd left him.

He was probably a dull man, a man who spent half his days with nails sticking out between his teeth, and the other half listening to polka shows on the radio. Except at nighttime when, as now, he listened to the radio call-in show that ran from midnight to dawn.

The woman continued to pant.

"Just thinking about it," she breathed, "I get— well, you know."

"So you say these Venusian guys, or whatever they were, drug you into the woods and had—how shall I put this delicately—had relations with you?"

"Many times. That night they had relations with me *many times!*"

Gus Fenster sat in the living room of his mobile home, creaking back and forth in his rocker, the radio on a stand he'd gotten at K-Mart a couple years back, the stand covered with a big white doilie that disguised the rings Gus' sweaty beer cans sometimes made.

He loved sitting in front of the radio like this.

Reminded him of when he was a kid.

All those great radio shows.

He'd always preferred, as now, listening in the dark, with the bright little face of the radio like a friendly night light.

Just rocking.

Sipping the generic beer he'd bought at the A&P.

Listening to this heavy-breathing woman talk about how the Venusians did it to her (she'd implied that the guys had been extremely well-endowed) and hoping that somebody would call in at least once tonight on the subject of buried treasure, that being Gus' favorite topic in all the world (the nights he bowled he liked to sit in the bar and talk buried-treasure stories with the other guys), buried treasure comprising half the story lines on his favorite radio shows of yesteryear, among them "Jack Armstrong" and "The Shadow." Even with tits bouncing up and down all the time, TV just didn't have the impact of those old radio shows.

This was what Gus was doing when the pick went into his lock.

When the pick turned left, then right, then left again.

When the chambers of the lock opened. A virgin offering herself at last.

Gus: just sitting there, as the door opened, all sound lost in the wind.

Just sitting there.

As the figure came up behind Gus.

As the hand flicked out, a perfect weapon, and caught Gus at the base of the neck.

Five minutes later the figure went back to the car and brought in the gasoline can.

By the time the car pulled away from the mobile-home court, flame had eaten its way up the drapes and begun spreading across the couch.

The radio was still on.

A second woman had called in, saying that the woman who'd been had by the Venusians had given her courage to tell her own story.

Alligator men had put the moves on her one night.

Gus sat in his chair.

Staring straight ahead.

Just staring, as the fire snapped at his pants and began charring his flesh.

As the woman on the radio said, "Just like alligators, they were. Just like 'em."

It was the kind of story Gus Fenster would have loved.

4

She ended up making them breakfast.

The refrigerator held a dozen eggs she hadn't used (hard to eat eggs when at least three times a week the newspaper made such an issue of cholesterol), some Smucker's strawberry jam, and an unopened quart of Minute Maid orange juice. From the vegetable keeper she took a green pepper and red onion, and with the eggs and paprika made them omelets.

"God," he said, "it's good to eat home cooking."

Diane smiled.

The Sonja Henie-John Payne movie had ended, and she had surprised herself by not being sleepy at all.

Indeed, his presence seemed to energize her, and she tried not to think about the implications of what her good mood meant.

He ate with pleasure and it gave her pleasure to watch him. Such a simple thing, sharing food, but it had been so long since she'd done it. Unless you counted wolfing down a Pizza Hut special on your dinner break with your deputy.

He must have sensed her pleasure, because when he looked up from his food, he said, "You cook very well."

"Thank you."

He looked around. "And I like your house."

"It's pretty small."

"Yeah, but it has personality."

"Thank you again."

His eyes fell on her.

"And I like you."

She knew she blushed.

Cheeks igniting.

At her age.

"Sounds like you're reading off a list," she joked.

"In a way, I am. I'm trying to tell you everything I feel without the aid of alcohol."

She nodded.

She hadn't offered him anything alcoholic to drink and he hadn't asked for anything, either. She had the sense that this was not his usual procedure at this time of night.

She felt pleased.

But she was also still embarrassed. So she said, a bit abruptly, "You mentioned something about having some news."

He smiled with a certain sadness. "So this festivity is going to degenerate into business, huh?"

"You've got me curious, is all."

"Well," he said, leaning back in his chair, looking up at the painting of a farm scene above the dining room table. It was an idyllic portrait of an idyllic life that, unfortunately, existed nowhere Diane Baines had ever been. "You know who Gus Fenster is?"

"I don't think so."

"A handyman. Free lance."

"Oh."

"He works for the Stockbridge organization. Old man Stockbridge handpicked him."

"Now I know I'll like him."

He laughed. "Your sarcasm isn't very subtle."

"I didn't intend it to be." She nodded. "Anyway—Gus Fenster."

"He called me earlier. About the death of Davie Mason." He shrugged. "For what it's worth, he doesn't think it was an accident."

The meal and the company had lulled her into a romantic mood. Now, with a single sentence, Tyler had changed that mood abruptly.

She said, "Is he a reliable sort? I mean, he doesn't—"

She stopped herself.

"No, he doesn't drink, at least not to excess like some people I know."

"I'm sorry. I—"

"Perfectly all right. Legitimate question coming from a sheriff."

For the second time that night she felt her face flush with embarrassment.

"Anyway," Tyler said, "he explained to me that there was nothing wrong with the step Davie Mason supposedly tripped on."

"Mind if I ask your opinion of what he's saying?"

"I think it's worth looking into."

She laughed. "I wish it were dawn. We could go see him."

"We can go see him now. He stays up all night and listens to this talk radio show."

"You mind?"

"Not at all."

* * *

"I suppose you wonder why I quit."

Five minutes later they were in Diane's patrol car. The seats were stiff with cold and they had to keep rubbing their gloved hands across the inside of the windshield to keep the frost from obscuring their vision. The car smelled of onions from the hamburger she'd had for lunch and vaguely of booze from a rather pathetic drunk she'd arrested a few nights ago.

"You already told me. Was there more to it?" she asked, then added, "You had a great reputation among the townspeople."

"Not all the townspeople."

"Nobody is universally loved, as one of my old college profs used to say."

"In this town you can be loved by everybody but one man, and if he doesn't like you, you're finished."

"Raymond Stockbridge?"

"Raymond Stockbridge."

"Why didn't he like you?"

"Well—what you asked me about earlier—the hit-and-run involving the boy named Peck from the orphanage?"

"Yes."

"Well, I had evidence, hard evidence, that the car involved belonged to Windhaven Orphanage."

"You're sure?"

"Absolutely."

"What happened to the evidence?"

"That's what I've always wanted to know." He looked outside. Trees stood like lonely sentries in the swirling snow. The car rocked occasionally from the wind. The yellow headlights lanced through the gloom. "I found the car that had been used. The fender showed the right kind of damage and there were traces of blood on the metal. I know because I had this verified by Doc Adams. I was afraid something might happen to the car—since it involved the Stockbridges and since the Stockbridges run the town—so I kept it in my garage. Then a funny thing happened."

"What?"

"My garage burned down. The car was charred beyond being useful."

"That must have been some fire."

"It was. A propane fire."

"You kept a propane tank in your garage?"

"That was one of those 'funny' little things nobody could ever explain to my satisfaction. There was no propane in my garage. Not until somebody put it there and started a fire with it, that is."

"My God," she said.

"Exactly."

5

He sat in the corner of the big dusty room like an animal that had been wounded and waited now only for his body to heal.

In the moonlight that fell through the dirty skylight he saw the bare wood floor and the piles of antiques, some of which dated back at least fifty years. The attic smelled of dust and cloth and mildew.

He sat with one hand idly playing with the object that had gotten him in trouble in the first place.

A tin soldier.

Darn her, anyway. Who did she think she was, putting him up here just because once in a while he—

But he didn't like to think about that—what he did sometimes.

Not that he meant to. Not that he planned it. It was just that—sometimes—without meaning to—he . . .

The swell of a massive trunk lay before him in the shadows. Then a torso form for fitting dresses.

So much junk.

He quit playing with the tin soldier now that his eyes penetrated the blackness and started to search in the corner. . . .

The corner under the eaves.

That was one place he didn't want to go.

That was one place he could never forget.

The corner.

Dim light fell on it now. Vaguely he could make out the shape.

The large urn, with Grecian writing on its side.

He put his head back down. No, he did not want to know about the corner. Or the urn there.

Or who had done the terrible thing to him.

He put his head back down and started playing with the tin soldier again. And started sobbing.

6

"My God!" John Tyler said. "Look!"

Gus Fenster's trailer, or rather what was left of it, sat on the edge of a clearing beneath the sprawling arms of two elm trees.

In the deep black night yellow-blue flames flicked against the ebon sky.

Forest animals stood in the melting snow around the periphery of the fire.

Diane jerked the car to a halt.

Tyler was out of the car and running toward the fiery mobile home before she could turn off the ignition.

What she saw in the next sixty seconds both terrified and impressed her.

Tyler tugged off his parka, threw it over his head, and ran headlong into the flames.

Above the noise of the fire and the keening of an approaching siren, she heard the screams of a man she presumed to be Gus Fenster. Her stomach became a twisted knot and she found herself muttering a Hail Mary.

The fire lit the night with an eerie brightness. Ironically, there was almost something beautiful about the sight—the majesty of the flames with the vast prairie night for a backdrop.

Hail Mary . . .

Tyler reappeared, dragging a body, just as the first fire engine from town ground through the blowing wall of snow, its red emergency lights stark in the gloom. Tyler laid the body of an older man on the snow and knelt beside him.

Closer sight of the old man reminded Diane of her experiences in morgues. She imagined that the charred flesh before her could be classified as third-degree burns. The *meatness* of the human body horrified her—the man looking little different from a steak that had been overdone, blood and juices flowing from the black-coated flesh.

She could see the truth. She wondered if Tyler who was working so desperately with the man, could see the same truth.

The man was dead.

Firemen, bulky in their rubber suits and awkward as Martians in their knee-high boots, uncoiled the hose line and began their job. Water was fired on the flames, splashing everywhere, freezing silver the moment it touched the air.

A fireman wearing a captain's hat came over to Diane.

"Gus Fenster, right, Sheriff?" the captain said.

"Right."

"And isn't that—" The captain, a Stockbridge flunky named Ries, looked at Tyler in disbelief. "Isn't that—?"

"Yes, it is, former Sheriff Tyler."

The captain shot her a serious look indeed. "He was never one of Raymond Stockbridge's favorite people."

"Is that a word of warning?"

"I was trying to be your friend, Diane," Ries said. "But I can see that you prefer a different type of person." He nodded to Tyler again. "Surprised he's sober enough even to stand up straight, this time of night."

With that, Ries went over to supervise his men.

Diane watched Tyler's last few minutes with the dead man. Finally, obviously shaken, he rose. At first he resembled a fighter who had been hit so hard he couldn't find his corner. Then he staggered through the snow, silhouetted against the flames, and wandered over to her.

He put out his hand and she could see he was crying. "I need a drink, Diane. I can't help it. They killed him. They fucking killed him."

"C'mon," she said, "I need a drink, too."

Chapter Six

1

For Elliot Hughes it had been another night with *Penthouse* behind the downstairs bathroom door.

Irna, his wife, had given up much if not all interest in sex ten years ago, right after the birth of their second child.

She had substituted, instead, an abiding interest in her husband's career at City Hall. The daughter of a failed mayoral candidate; failed, in fact, three different times, Irna had determined early that the only way a career could be advanced in Haversham was by doing what her father had never done—getting along with Raymond Stockbridge.

Her father had seen Stockbridge as selfish, corrupt, evil. And Stockbridge had crushed her father, and in so doing had quite literally killed him. The night after losing on his third try, her father had asphyxiated himself.

When she'd found him, a few hours later, he had looked like an animal that had been trying to claw his way free of imprisonment. His hands had raked the fumy air, his eyes bulging imploringly. A prayer had seemed to form roundly on his pink mouth.

Instead of shrieking in horror, Irna, then twelve years old and the only girl at Stockbridge Junior High to win both a Sweetheart Ball accolade and a Science Merit Award, simply looked down at her father in disgust for being the weakling he was. In movies people were always noble about committing suicide. Violins swelled as guns were put to temples—noble. But this man, her father—

Disgusting.

She spent the rest of her life trying to live down the foolish things her father had done with his life.

Her first opportunity to make amends came when she was a senior in high school. The event was an essay contest for which the winner would receive a full-ride one-year scholarship to the state university.

The title of Irna's essay was, "Why Raymond Stockbridge Is Our Own George Washington." The night she read her prize-winning piece to an appreciative high school audience (seeing as they were seated in the Raymond Stockbridge Gymnasium, only a stone's throw from Stockbridge High, they had darned well better be appreciative), Mr. Stockbridge himself could be seen to tear up fulsomely. This night was remarkable for another event, too. On the evening of May 29, 1958, she finally let Elliot Hughes, her steady boyfriend, slide his sweaty hand all the way down inside the heart-covered panties her mother had gotten for her last

118

birthday at Penny's.

It was the beginning of a very serious romance.

Only occasionally did Elliot think of these things when he snuck down to the bathroom on the first floor. He always made sure the kids were asleep. He always made sure Irna was asleep. He always made sure Brownie, their collie, was asleep.

Then he crept down the stairs, *Penthouse* in hand, went to the bathroom, and pleasured himself.

Once in a while he'd remember how it had once been with Irna (the sexy way her breasts hung when she was on top of him, the slope of her buttocks in the moonlight) and that would make him slightly crazy (in the way nostalgia always makes people crazy— you yearn so hard for what used to be that you fail to have much respect for the people and things around you now). But then he'd quickly get back to the *Penthouse*, to the bountiful women with their legs spread and their sweet little pink lips waiting for him.

Tonight, howling, blowing though it was— tonight was such a night.

He had risen carefully from the bed so as not to wake Irna; he had crept past the sprawled and snoring form of Brownie; he had eased past the bedroom door leading to the kids' room; he had taken his magazine from the official briefcase he kept in the upstairs closet; and he was halfway down the stairs, thinking of the Italian woman in the centerfold ("From experience, Sophia has learned that just because a man isn't a strapping hulk doesn't mean he's not all man"—and wasn't that a perfect description of Elliot—no strapping hulk, to be sure,

119

but ALL MAN, nonetheless). He was halfway down the stairs, stealthy as a crook in a Disney cartoon, when it happened.

The phone rang.

Him in his underwear.

With a *Penthouse* in his hand.

("Mommy, why does Daddy have that dirty magazine in his hands?")

("Go back to bed now, children. I'm going to have a little talk with your father.")

("YOU SICK, PERVERTED BEAST! WHAT KIND OF EXAMPLE ARE YOU SETTING FOR YOUR OWN CHILDREN! IN YOUR UNDERWEAR, MY GOD!, IN YOUR UNDERWEAR!")

Throughout the house, lights flew up.

Brownie began roaring.

And within moments, Irna stood, a hair-curlered empress with matronly ire crackling in her gaze, staring at a man she obviously had no more respect for than she'd had for her father.

"May I ask what that is in your hand?" she inquired.

The phone continued to ring.

"Shouldn't we get the phone, honey?" he asked.

"Shut up! I asked you what that is in your hand."

"*Time* magazine."

The phone continued to ring.

"Honey, shouldn't we get the—"

But she was down the stairs and ripping the magazine out of his hands before he could say anything else.

"Just look at this!" she cried. "Just look at this!"

Biff and Buffy, the children, stood at the top of the

stairs in matching pullover pajamas, rubbing beady eyes with tiny fists, amused as always when Mommy was reaming Daddy a new one.

She slapped him with it, then threw it at him and fled up the steps, back to her room, the pieces of torn magazine floating to the floor like dying birds.

The phone stopped ringing.

He stood there immobilized, Biff and Buffy still staring at him.

And then Irna came back, ashen. But her voice lilted. Instead of a shriek there was now a song. That could mean only one thing.

That whoever was on the phone was indeed an important personage.

He was not a man of self-confidence. He fled up the steps fast, as she had.

He was always expecting a call, middle of the night, just like this, with a mystery voice intoning, "Elliot, we've found out about you. We know that secretly you're a total incompetent and must be put out of office immediately."

He pressed the receiver to his ear, the feelings of the last few moments—terror, humiliation, rage—subtracting at least three months from his lifespan.

"Yes?" he said, hoping for good news; but who would call in the middle of the night with good news?

"Good evening, Mayor."

No doubt about who the voice belonged to.

Sweaty as he was from all the excitement, Elliot shivered.

"Good evening," he said.

She got right to it. But then Mrs. Kilrane always

did. "There is somebody who wants to make our lives very difficult."

"Who?"

"Can you come out to the orphanage?"

"Of course. How about nine tomorrow morning?"

"I mean right now."

"Right now!"

"Yes, Mayor." She paused. "Right now."

Then she hung up.

Obviously displeased.

After she hung up, another receiver was also replaced.

That would be Irna on the extension.

She appeared moments later.

"Very nice, Elliot. Very nice."

The edge in her voice indicated that she was as unhappy as Mrs. Kilrane.

"She wanted you to be enthusiastic. She wanted you to say, 'I'll be right out, Mrs. Kilrane.' But no, you couldn't do that, could you, Elliot? You couldn't act like a real man for once and do your duty. No, you had to whine and moan and finally make her angry before you agreed to go out there." She shook her head. "Is that the kind of man the voters want, Elliot? Don't they want somebody strong and tireless and always eager to serve them?"

"Honey, my hemorrhoids are really bad tonight," he said.

"That didn't stop you from taking that filthy magazine downstairs."

"Honey, maybe if we, if you—"

"You're going to blame me? Oh, my God, Elliot, you're going to blame me for your perversions? Has it crossed your mind that I'd be more willing to share my favors with you if you acted more like a man? If you were more eager to do what the Stockbridge family wants you to do?"

"But Irna, you know people laugh at me now. They think I do *too* much for the Stockbridge family."

"Not 'people,' Elliot, scum. Sick, envious scum who are always complaining. Always complaining." She looked at him with a certain sadness. "Now, Elliot, you go over there and do what Mrs. Kilrane wants you to do, whatever that is, and when you come back here I'll be waiting up for you."

She came to him and kissed him. Her breath was sweet from Colgate and the swell of her breasts was warm and soft.

He got one of those erections that make you insane with frustration.

With a single finger sharp as a ruler, she thwacked it down for him.

"No time for that now. You get over to Mrs. Kilrane's."

A few minutes later he was out in the night, thankful for the sense of isolation the gloom and the swirling snow gave him.

Perhaps he would get lost.

Forever.

2

The sky was changing from the ebon cloud-scudded wall above the earth to a bruised dawn that gave the earth below an alien aspect.

Brian sat by the window, staring out at the swampy area. He wore a sweater and a heavy shirt and a t-shirt. He felt as if his body temperature were twenty degrees below normal.

Only occasionally did he stare at his hand.

He wanted to will it from existence.

All his life Brian had dreaded that he was a freak, being different from the normal, self-confident boys he had known. And tonight, the incident at the swamp had proved that his fears were true. His eyes returned to it now. It was nothing more than a swamp, black and bleak in the yellow light of alien sky.

He put his hand up to the window and scrutinized it carefully. Now, it was nothing more than the hand of a twelve-year-old boy named Brian. Nothing special at all. Certainly no beams of searing light shot from it.

Curiously, he used his other hand to touch the finger where the beam had come from. Nothing. He bit his nails so the fingernail looked rough. There was a scratch from where he'd been playing with a cat. And there was a bruise he'd gotten playing basketball. Otherwise, nothing.

An everyday, ordinary twelve-year-old finger.

Then, almost against his will, he pointed the finger at the handle of the closet across from him. He wondered, with a mixture of fascination and dread, if he could call up the power at his own discretion. . . .

He closed his eyes and concentrated hard. He willed all his mind and soul into his one finger.

And then—

He opened his eyes.

It was almost funny.

He felt as if an adult had caught him with a bathrobe wound around his neck playing Superman or something. His finger had about as much power as a stick you picked up off the ground.

He went back to staring out the window. For a time he forgot his concerns about the swamp, about Davie Mason's voice calling him. Instead he thought of something infinitely more frightening—the fact that Caroline would be leaving him soon for her new adoptive parents. And even though the sun began to peek through the winter murk of the dawning sky, his spirits sank.

He was closer to Caroline than he'd ever been to anyone and now—

Anger over being deserted again—as he had been by his parents, and even by the one dog he'd called his own—anger rose in him.

He continued to sit at the window, staring outside.

But his hand came away from the frosty pane, came away and lowered into the position it had been in previously, aimed directly at the doorknob on the closet.

Down the hall came the sounds of the first boys stirring in the morning.

Curses, laughter, shouts.

Even further away he could hear doors opening and closing. Feet stamping off snow in the vestibule downstairs. Heavy men moving heavily through the orphanage. The cooks come to start breakfast.

And then it happened.

A searing scorch of flame and—

The doorknob ripped away and fell to the floor.

As he had at the swamp, he stared in wonderment and horror at his own powers. This was impossible. And yet—

The sensation of boiling blood coursing through him came again, as if he had been seized by a fever.

The anger.

That was what had done it.

When he wasn't angry, the powers wouldn't come to him.

But now—he sank to the floor, terrified.

"Are you really sure you want this, John?" Diane Baines asked the man across from her at the dining room table.

"No. I wouldn't say I'm 'sure' I want it. But the idea of it sounds awfully good, I have to say that."

Just after leaving the fire, the fire that had killed Gus Fenster, the idea of a drink had sounded reasonable to Diane. Tyler was under a lot of stress, and surely that was a fair time to have a drink. But on the way back to her place she had started thinking about his obvious problem with alcohol and whether or not she would be doing him a favor.

She had gone so far as to put a quart of Budweiser from the fridge on the table between them, along with two glasses.

But now she had second thoughts.

"How about a cup of coffee?"

He stared at the sweating quart bottle. "You think I'm an alcoholic, don't you?"

"I think there's that possibility," she said, gently.

He sighed, looking very old at that moment.

"I wish I could describe to you how I feel right now," he said.

"Try."

He sighed again. "I don't know if I can."

At the dining room window the new day pressed

like a curtain of gold.

"Please," she said again, "try. I'm a good listener."

He smiled. "You're good at a lot of things."

"Thank you."

"I liked him."

"Gus?"

"Yes."

"From how you've described him, I think I would have liked him, too."

"He reminded me a lot of my own father."

His fist came down like a boulder.

The whole table shook.

He sat across from her, raw in his rage and pain.

"That's how they've been running Haversham for years!" he exploded. "If somebody gets in your way—kill them!"

"We have to allow for one possibility," she said. She spoke barely above a whisper so she wouldn't sound as if she were questioning his integrity. "There is an off chance that the fire was a coincidence, a real accident."

"No way!"

And with that, he brought his fist down again.

He reached out for the bottle, seizing it by the neck as if it were some kind of animal he needed to tame. He looked at her with his dark, injured gaze, and she saw many things in the man—shame and helplessness and an anger that had been there a long time.

"You don't want me to, do you?" he said, nodding to the bottle.

"It's your decision."

"But you'd rather I didn't?"

"I'd rather you wouldn't."

His fingers left the bottle.

He got up and started pacing. He had begun to sweat and his eyes looked a bit wild.

She let him go, just watched him.

Finally, he turned to her and said, "I'm going home and take a shower and put on fresh clothes and then I'm going to see Stockbridge."

His decision had calmed him, his determination given him a peace.

She started to stand up, but he stopped her by leaning down and kissing her.

Her first impulse was to push him gently away. While she liked him, felt an unmistakable attraction to him, the events of the past twelve hours had left her confused and feeling vulnerable. She wasn't sure where her relationship with John Tyler might go—and thinking back to her failed marriage, the prospect of what lay ahead frightened her.

But finally she didn't stop him.

It was a chaste kiss, really, as much friendly as passionate, but behind it there was certainly the promise of animal urgency.

When he pulled back, she was reluctant to let him go. In his arms she had felt his loss—a loss not unlike hers—and she drew an odd strength from it. She felt less lonely than she had for years.

"I'll go with you to see Stockbridge," she said.

"Are you kidding?"

"No."

"He'll fire you."

"That's inevitable, anyway."

He slid his arm around her. "Just because we—I mean—"

"I know what you mean. But that's not the reason I'm doing it. I've felt there was something wrong with the story the orphanage put out about the Mason boy right from the start. Don't forget that I'm sheriff. I'm only doing my duty as I see it."

He slid his arm around her. "I can't believe my luck in meeting you."

She smiled.

Then watched his eyes.

They fell to the Budweiser.

"You can put that back in the refrigerator if you want, right now."

"I could even pour it out." She put a smile on her words, but it was obvious she was being serious.

"Hey," he laughed. "I'm not taking the pledge. I don't know if I'm strong enough for that. I'm not even sure I want to do it. But for right now I don't want it. Okay?"

"Great."

He kissed her on the cheek and said, "I'll be back for you in about an hour."

"Fine. That'll give me a chance to freshen up, too."

After he left, she put the beer away and sat in the kitchen. It was at times like these that she wanted a cigarette, a habit she'd given up five years ago.

She felt such a turmoil of emotions—

She shrugged, smiled. If he could pass up a drink, she could certainly pass up a cigarette.

She had just gone into the bathroom to run shower water when she heard a car door slam in her driveway.

130

She went to the window and looked out.

At the unmistakable black limousine.

And the unmistakable figure emerging slowly, and with great effort, from the back seat.

Raymond Stockbridge.

A chill of terror went through her.

4

Caroline bumped him with her tray to get his attention.

Brian turned around in the cafeteria line and stared at her.

For a moment, she saw something in his eyes she'd never noticed before.

Something she didn't like.

Not at all.

The same kind of anger her real father used to show just as he was about to beat her.

She was so surprised by his look, she almost dropped her tray.

Fortunately, the look vanished as quickly as it had come up.

They finished their slow passage through the line—Caroline, hungry, getting eggs, bacon, toast, milk, orange juice, and a small box of Rice Krispies—and finally found a table near the back.

She could not take her eyes from him.

It was like trying to put a puzzle together. She sensed that he had changed somehow, in some subtle but profound way, and tried to decide exactly what the process of change meant.

Abruptly, he said, "Why are you staring at me?"

"Because I like you."

"That's not why and you know it."

"Because I'm scared."

"Of what?"

"Of what happened back there at the swamp last night."

"Forget last night."

"But, Brian—"

"I said forget last night." This time the anger was in his voice as well as his eyes.

"But—"

Mr. Rydell passed by. "You don't look any the worse for wear, Caroline." He smiled his vaguely unpleasant smile. "Sleepwalking must agree with you."

Then he was gone.

When her gaze returned to Brian, she saw for the first time that his normally open, friendly eyes appeared to have receded, as if his brow were trying to conceal them. She shuddered.

"I want to help you, Brian."

"I don't want your help."

She could not believe what she had just heard.

"What?"

"I don't want your help."

"But Brian, we're friends. We're—"

He jerked away from the table and stood up. Then he strode across the cafeteria and out the door. All she could do was sit there and watch him in disbelief.

Mayor Elliot Hughes walked into Mrs. Kilrane's office with the air of a pet about to be severely reprimanded. She sat behind the massive desk where her father sometimes put himself and watched Hughes come into the room.

"There's going to be trouble about the Mason boy," she said.

"What kind of trouble?"

He was not a man capable of handling difficult situations. While this made him ideal as a puppet, it made him less than ideal as somebody to rely on.

"Sheriff Baines and former Sheriff Tyler were seen together last night." Her tone implied that she found anything that might have gone on between the two absolutely disgusting. "Earlier yesterday, Gus Fenster had talked to Tyler. He was giving Tyler reason to raise questions about the death—the same way he raised questions fifteen years ago."

"Maybe I could speak to Gus," the mayor said blandly.

"He's already been taken care of."

"I'm not sure what you mean."

"There was a fire at his trailer."

The mayor's eyes widened. "You mean he's dead?"

"Yes, Mayor," she said sarcastically, "I mean he's dead."

"My God. What if—?"

"What if somebody finds out? That's where you come in. The fire captain is going to spend the next few days investigating the fire. He's going to conclude that it was quite accidental. And you're going to make a public statement about believing him. And then help close the matter."

"But what if there are more questions?"

There was a certain snakelike grace with which Mrs. Kilrane rose from behind the desk.

"If there are more questions, we'll deal with them."

He shook his head miserably.

A fire guttered in the fireplace and an FM tuner played Mozart. Daylight splashed on the leather spines of hundreds of books. Everything in this room smacked of civilization, of culture. Everything but Mrs. Kilrane.

She came around the desk with menacing energy. "I need your help in getting rid of our sheriff. . . ."

"Sheriff Baines?"

Mrs. Kilrane smiled nastily. Daylight filled her eyeglasses so that her eyes were obscured. "You're babbling, Mayor. Of course, Sheriff Baines."

"But she's a woman."

"Really? I hadn't noticed."

"I just mean that—because she's a woman and all—we can't—well, we couldn't treat her—"

"How touching."

The mayor flushed.

"How touching that you'd have so much concern for her just because of her gender."

The mayor kept his eyes on the floor. He knew

135

Mrs. Kilrane was humiliating him. Much as his wife humiliated him. Much as many people in the town of Haversham humiliated him.

He thought longingly of the days when he'd been a hardware clerk. He thought longingly of the widow woman who'd also worked in the store . . . Emma Simpson.

Why couldn't his life have stayed that simple? Why had his wife forced him to run for mayor?

When he looked up again, he saw that Mrs. Kilrane was holding something out for him.

A small plastic bag with white powder . . .

When he realized what she was proposing, something terrible happened to the mayor's stomach.

"Oh, no," he said.

The nasty smile returned. "Be a man for once, Mayor. Be a man and do your duty."

Mrs. Kilrane sounded like a speaker at a Kiwanis Club meeting.

"But she isn't that kind of woman, and nobody would believe—"

Mrs. Kilrane held up a halting hand. "These days, Mayor, everybody will believe anything about anybody. There's so much scandal that nobody's safe. Just start a rumor about somebody and no matter how false it might be, within a day you find the majority of the people believing." She shook her mannish head. "We'll have no problem with the sheriff. She'll know that she has no choice but to resign gracefully."

"But somebody will see me putting it in her car. People will recognize me."

Mrs. Kilrane put herself on the edge of her desk.

Her sarcasm was gone. She seemed to be regarding the mayor as if he were a retarded child. *"You* won't put it in her car. You'll get somebody to do it for you."

All he could think of was Emma Simpson and the day in the back room of the hardware store when she'd let him . . .

The mayor wondered if dying would be like this . . . vivid pleasant images in your mind so that you didn't have to confront . . .

"You'll get Deputy Farnsworth to help you."

"Deputy Farnsworth? But he's one of her best friends."

From a humidor Mrs. Kilrane took a long, slim cigarillo, smelled its aroma, then put it between her lips.

"Let's just say that I have 'persuaded' Farnsworth to help us," she said in a confidential manner. "So you see there's really nothing whatsoever to worry about, Mayor."

She handed him the cocaine.

He had never seen the stuff in real life before. Only on "Miami Vice," a show he had to watch in the rec room downstairs on the little black-and-white set because his wife thought the language on the program was horrible.

In the palm of his hand the white stuff burned with the power of hell.

"There's something I need to know, Mrs. Kilrane."

She looked amused that he'd be questioning her. "Yes?"

"Why are we doing this?"

"Getting rid of Sheriff Baines?"

He nodded.

"Because she is about to make a very vile accusation."

"I see."

He sweated.

"Mrs. Kilrane," he went on, souding as tortured as if somebody had been pounding nails into his feet, "Mrs. Kilrane, as mayor, maybe I'd better be informed about what that accusation might be."

The sneer was back on her lips. She glanced down at her cigarillo, then back up at him. "Are you challenging me, Mayor?"

He gulped.

He could just hear his wife if he told her that he'd argued with Mrs. Kilrane.

"No," he said.

"Too bad," she smiled. "And here I was hoping you were getting some balls."

"I just thought that—well—as mayor, I mean—"

She got down from the edge of the desk. Walked several paces toward him.

He backed up until there was no place for him to go. His back was against the door.

"Do you find me attractive, Mayor?"

My God! he thought. How do I answer this one? It was the worst trick question he'd ever heard of.

If he said yes, she could accuse him of coming on to her.

If he said no, she could accuse him of being insulting.

She pushed herself closer, parting her lips so that he saw teeth so white they looked capped, the way a movie star's might look.

Despite himself, he felt the first stirrings of an erection. With Mrs. Kilrane!

"Well?" she said.

Then the phone rang.

The mayor almost broke out laughing and crying at the same time.

Mrs. Kilrane saw the relief on his face and resented him for it.

"We'll take this up at another time," she said, the nasty smile returning to her lips.

The mayor slipped out quickly as possible, the cocaine impossibly heavy in the jacket of his suitcoat.

6

The whole house seemed a tilt when Raymond Stockbridge stepped up on the porch.

With his size, his passage up the walk had been so slow that whole hours had seemed to pass while Diane waited for him to appear.

Or rather: them—Raymond Stockbridge was not alone.

She recognized the woman accompanying him as Mrs. B.D. Exter, wife of the local bank president. A matronly woman in her early fifties, she was active in many causes, not the least of which was Women for Good Government. She was known to be a staunch enemy of Diane's, believing that a female sheriff was not "feminine." At a Good Government meeting Mrs. Exter had suggested that Diane made the prisoners "crazy" because her body inspired lust. Diane had laughed it off as a weird sort of compliment (she was attractive enough, but hardly a sexpot) but she knew that Mrs. Exter was little more than a stalking horse for the Stockbridge family. They wanted to be rid of Diane at the end of her term.

Mrs. Exter sniffed the air as if there had been a recent sewage spill.

Raymond Stockbridge eyed the sheriff with his usual mixture of desire and derision.

"We would like to talk to you," Stockbridge said.

Even that short of a sentence caused his breath to come in short gasps. He made Orson Welles look svelte.

"Of course," she said.

Diane was sensible enough to be alarmed. What was going on here, anyway?

They came in and she found them seats (Raymond Stockbridge taking the couch by himself, covering nearly half of it once he was seated), offered them coffee, which they declined, and sat perched on the edge of her chair like a nervous child expecting scolding.

Mrs. Exter began. "As you know, I am the President of Women for Good Government."

Diane nodded.

"And as such, it is my responsibility to listen to all complaints about our officials." She smiled in the direction of Raymond Stockbridge. "Fortunately, I am happy to say, there are very few complaints, thanks to the careful screening our officials receive."

Diane took deep breaths. They didn't help. Her heart pounded. Her hands sweated. All she could do was nod.

"Recently, both Mr. Stockbridge and myself have had to listen to certain stories about you, Ms. Baines."

Ms. never "Sheriff Baines." Mrs. Exter had always made it clear that she considered that title unseemly when applied to a woman.

"What about me?" Diane asked. She could not keep the edge out of her voice. Knowing everything she knew about this town, it was hard not to be angry when gossip was spread about you.

141

"Well," Mrs. Exter said primly, "perhaps I'd better let Mr. Stockbridge explain."

Stockbridge leaned forward on his cane, like some emperor contemplating his subjects.

"This is not an accusation, you understand," he began. "We're simply trying to get to the bottom of the rumor."

"What rumor?"

"That you're a drug addict."

Under other conditions, Diane would have burst out laughing. But with the deaths of Davie Mason and Gus Fenster on her mind, nothing struck her as funny.

"That's absurd," she said.

"Nonetheless, it's a story we're hearing more and more often these days."

"Well, it's ridiculous." She hated the tone of her voice, the whining note. She wished more than ever that she could have a cigarette.

"I'd like to know who has accused me," she said.

"That would hardly be proper," Mrs. Exter said.

"Oh, but it's proper to make any kind of accusation you like, with nothing more than malice or hearsay behind it—that's 'proper,' I suppose?"

Obviously Mrs. Exter did not like being talked to that way.

Diane tried to calm herself.

She looked around at all the familiar objects in the house. The fabric wall hangings, last remnants of her hippie days. The record collection that ran from Jefferson Starship to Verdi. The china cabinet that had belonged to her parents; it made her sentimental just to look at it.

She looked back at them. "I don't take drugs," she said.

"You totally deny the accusation?"

"Totally."

"Good," said Raymond Stockbridge. He put on the air of a judge who was closing a case. "Then I can report this to the council, which meets in just an hour, and maybe things will be put in order then."

Mrs. Exter stood up.

From her expression it was obvious she did not approve of Diane's little house any more than she approved of Diane herself.

"I'll be happy to submit to blood tests or any other kind of medical evaluation," Diane said.

"And we appreciate that," Raymond Stockbridge said.

Within the folds of his massive overcoat, his weight moved upward so that, with great difficulty, he stood next to Mrs. Exter.

"We'll get this resolved," he said in a manner meant to be comforting.

That was one thing that Diane had never quite fathomed about Stockbridge. For all his menacing power, his presence seemed largely ceremonial, as if he were only the representative for somebody else. Diane wondered who that might be.

Mrs. Exter drew a finger over the stereo cabinet and looked at the dust she'd gathered. "Very nice house you have here," she announced.

Her sarcasm was not lost on any of them.

*   *   *

Minutes after they left, Diane dialed John Tyler's number.

"We don't need to see Stockbridge," she said.

"Why?"

"He just left."

"What did he want?"

"I'm not sure. But I'm beginning to get an inkling. Somebody has accused me of being a drug addict."

"That's a good way to discredit any inquiries you might make about the Mason boy's death."

"Exactly."

"They're really moving in, aren't they?"

"Yes, I'm afraid they are."

Chapter Seven

1

The basement was a place of cobwebs and mildew, of odors like cider, dust, and dampness.

Having cut his first class, Brian stood in the basement, ready to experiment again with what he'd learned earlier that morning.

He stood facing a metal tool box. Staring at it. He closed his eyes and blanked his mind much as possible, then waited to receive thoughts from the swamp.

Nothing came.

Then he allowed his own thoughts to form—images of Caroline, of his onetime dog, of his posters and records and books. And slowly, like a piece of music distantly heard, the headache began.

At first Brian chose not to recognize it.

The power he'd displayed last night—the tree branch ripping off in flames—still haunted him. He had felt such a great release when his rage against Windhaven had filled him and had been expressed in that sudden surge of power, but— But still it was frightening.

Ineluctably, however, certain thoughts came to his mind, the bitter memories of a bitter boy.

The foster home where a gruff man had beaten him in drunk delight.

The earlier orphanage where an older boy had bullied and humiliated him at every opportunity.

The public school where some of the children had drawn his name on the board and written dirty things after it.

Finally, he thought of Windhaven, of his dead friend Davie Mason, of Mrs. Kilrane, of the ominous threat of Mr. Stockbridge.

The headache grew.

The impression of metal bands tightening across his skull returned.

As his rage grew, so did the pain.

Brian—

He had no doubt now where the voice came from. The swamp.

Brian—

He staggered toward the metal tool box, slamming his hands over his head. It was like the other nights— whorls of colors before his eyes—a feeling that his own body was bursting with a horrible energy—

Brian—

Images of Windhaven in flames played across his mind again.

He sensed he had only one way to stop the forces

that tried to possess him now. Good thoughts. He forced himself to picture Caroline in his mind. Sweet, patient, understanding Caroline. At first it did no good, but then he fought against his headache—it was as if he were dueling with his own consciousness—and finally a wispy picture of Caroline formed before his eyes. He felt the headache lessen slightly. She became even more vivid—and the headache receded even more.

BRIAN—

The voice completely obliterated all else in Brian's mind. Power overcame him and his gaze fell on the tool box.

The metal box burst into flame, melting into a twisted smoking piece of scrap.

During science class, Caroline wrote down her prayer request on a piece of notebook paper.

She had learned long ago that God liked things written down in the best penmanship possible. It was ever so much more impressive than simply asking for something mentally. Everybody asked for something, but few took the time to write down what they wanted.

So she sat at her desk, sinking down in her seat, writing in a clear hand the words:

PLEASE TAKE BRIAN'S POWERS.
THEY WILL JUST GET HIM IN TROUBLE.

Then her eyes strayed over to the empty seat where

147

Brian should have been. She did not like to think of what he might be doing. She still felt terrible—cold, totally alone—when she thought of how he'd looked at her this morning when he'd said that he didn't want any of her help. When he obviously could have cared less if she lived or died.

Brian.

Her boyfriend.

Her best friend.

Not caring if she lived or died, and all because of his new powers.

As she sat there, the sunlight making a fire of the autumnal hills in the distance, the classroom smelling lazily of furniture polish and chalk dust, she thought of last night's events. Of the cold blue light at the bottom of the swamp. Of the voice that had taken over Brian. Even though she hadn't been able to hear it, she'd certainly witnessed its effects, so there was no doubt of its reality.

"Miss Hayes."

She heard her name only dimly at first.

"Miss Hayes."

Again. Her name. But she didn't quite connect it with herself.

"MISS HAYES!"

Angry, this time, Mrs. Kenrod's voice.

When she looked up, she saw that Mrs. Kenrod hovered over her.

"May I see that piece of paper please?"

Caroline paled. Gathering all her strength, knowing that all her classmates were watching, Caroline sat up straight.

She looked up at the squat gray-haired woman with the thick eyeglasses and said, "No."

Mrs. Kenrod looked as if somebody had struck her. "You're refusing to do what I ask?"

"Yes."

"Hand that piece of paper over here, Caroline, and right now."

"I can't, Mrs. Kenrod. I'd like to, but I can't."

"That's an order, Caroline. An order."

"I know."

Usually Caroline was disliked by her classmates because she was so cooperative with teachers.

The laughter that spread among the other kids was as much out of shock as anything.

Caroline Hayes refusing to obey a teacher.

What a riot.

Mrs. Kenrod's hand shot out, palm up.

"Put that piece of paper in my hand. Right this instant."

All Caroline could do was shake her head.

Mrs. Kenrod slapped Caroline hard across the mouth.

Caroline gasped. It felt as if her whole head was numb.

"The paper," Mrs. Kenrod said.

Before another blow could be landed, Caroline jumped up and fled the room.

Laughter and shouts followed her.

She could hear Mrs. Kenrod shouting for order.

Caroline only wished that order might be returned to her own heart. When she reached the hall, she burst into tears and started running, her penny

149

loafers slapping the marble floor, faster than she ever had in her life.

After finishing in the basement, Brian went upstairs to his room and took a nap. His tension had cost him a great deal of strength.

He came awake bathed in sweat and sensing a presence in the room.

The beautiful if unlikely November sunlight fell on Caroline Hayes who stood just inside the door, watching him.

"Are you all right?" she asked.

For the moment all he could do was stare, trying to rid himself of the afterbirth of nightmare.

She came closer.

"Are you, Brian? Are you all right?"

He found his voice. It was squeaky. Much younger than he usually sounded. "Yes." Then he realized what would happen if she were found in his room. Mrs. Kilrane became psychopathic when boys and girls were found in each other's rooms. "You've got to get out of here."

"I need to talk to you first."

"Somewhere else."

"No."

The strength of her voice surprised Brian.

She put out a hand. Pushed it against his shoulder. Holding him still for a moment.

"You scared me this morning. The way you looked. The way you talked."

Now that he'd had some sleep, he recalled the scene

she referred to with some confusion. She was right, of course. He had treated her badly. Something had come over him. A flame-burning anger that had obscured all else and had held him in an unbreakable grip.

Caroline—of all people to treat badly.

"I'm sorry," he said.

"Oh, God."

"What?"

But before he could even attempt to understand the situation, she sat down on the bed and hugged him.

"I was scared, Brian. I thought you didn't want me as your friend anymore."

When she started to cry, Brian had no idea what to do. He started to pat her awkwardly on the arm while she told him what had happened in class. Then he heard the unmistakable sounds of Mr. Rydell's crepe soles coming down the hall.

"God," Caroline said.

"Quick," Brian said.

He pushed her under the bed.

He was sweating, blushing, and shaking by the time Mr. Rydell poked his head in.

"Did I hear you talking to somebody, Brian?"

"Huh-uh, Mr. Rydell."

The teacher looked around suspiciously. "Are you sure?"

"I'm sure."

"Why aren't you in class?"

"The flu."

"You've been to see Nurse Ament?"

"No, but I know I've got it. My head hurts and my

151

stomach hurts and I've been throwing up."

Brian had such a powerful imagination that as he described his symptoms, he began to feel them.

"You know you need a written excuse from Nurse Ament."

By now Brian had a croaky voice. "Soon as I feel better, I'll go down there."

Mr. Rydell smirked. "You must be feeling reasonably well, Brian."

"Why's that?"

"You're wearing your shoes. Most people who are sick in bed don't wear their shoes."

With that, letting Brian know that his story had been less than convincing, Mr. Rydell took one more look around the room, then left.

"God," Caroline said when she came out from under the bed.

"You want to go someplace with me?"

"Where?"

"Into town."

"For what?"

"A trip to the library."

"Mrs. Kilrane will kill us."

"We're already in trouble. Both of us."

Then she smiled and said, "Sure. Why not?"

Brian got off the bed and smiled at her. You couldn't ask for a better friend than Caroline. He tried to stop himself from thinking of how, in less than two weeks, she'd be gone.

He got out his parka and they left.

Mr. Rydell waited around the far corner, watching

as Brian and Caroline snuck down the hall toward the backstairs.

Mr. Rydell had to smile to himself.

They moved with a stealth that was almost theatrical, almost comic.

He almost felt bad that he had to spy on them this way.

2

In the cloakroom hung pictures of various American presidents, beginning with the inevitable George Washington and ending with the not-so-inevitable Jimmy Carter.

Only occasionally did cloakroom visitors pause to look at these portraits, and only one president was ever commented on, that being the timeless and tireless Harry S. Truman. Today the cloakroom smelled of snow and pipe smoke and cold as a dozen men trooped in and out, leaving puddles on the floor and wraiths of Cherrywood pipe tobacco in the air.

Around the corner from the cloakroom was the City Council chambers. Members sat at an inverted U of a desk. People presenting cases sat in chairs in the curve of the U. The inquisitional nature of the arrangement was obvious and, from the council members' point of view, useful.

The east wall was hung with large black-and-white framed photos of Haversham at various stages of its growth. In some you saw Model Ts with people in straw boaters grinning at the camera. In others were grim-faced youths debarking a Greyhound bus in 1942, on their way from boot camp to possible death in Europe or the jungles of South America. The closer the photos got to the present, the more one saw of Raymond Stockbridge—"more" in all senses.

154

For one thing, each photo showed him with additional weight. A handsome if nondescript man was transformed over a twenty-year period into a blimp of a man. Only the harsh judgment of the eyes kept him from being comic. Inevitably he was portrayed as a Santa Claus figure. Here he performed groundbreaking duties at a shopping center—here he handed out relief packs to residents whose homes had been flooded—here he balanced a small girl on one knee and a teddy bear on the other. And so on.

It was only when one looked carefully that a second pattern in the more recent photos could be seen. Starting from the time she was a nearsighted, pigtailed, knock-kneed girl of eight, Mrs. Kilrane (who at one time had endured the name Brandy Lou Stockbridge) could be seen in each photograph. There were eight photographs, comprising a time span of fourteen years, and Mrs. Kilrane evolved in them from a gawky girl to a severe and in some ways sexless young woman whose eyes radiated a malevolent kind of beauty. Whatever the circumstances of the photograph, those eyes stabbed out at you, beaconlike, stunning. Except for the final photograph, when their terrible clarity was hidden beyond thick eyeglasses of the sort librarians are supposed to wear but never, in fact, do.

Moving one's gaze down from that photograph this morning, one could see the owner of that strange gaze in the flesh. In the chair in the exact center of the U, in the huge chair where her father usually resided, sat Mrs. Kilrane.

The other members of the council looked at each other nervously. They did not have to be told that her presence here was a bad sign.

Mrs. Kilrane lifted the gavel and brought it down. The meeting came to order.

"Gentlemen," she said coldly, "I am here today for a simple reason. My father has taken ill."

"I hope it's nothing serious," Mr. Sale, the toadying old department store owner whined.

Mrs. Kilrane knew exactly what he really meant. In his heart of hearts he wished that Mr. Stockbridge, tyrant, ogre, fiend, would fall down dead.

As they all wished he did.

Mrs. Kilrane said, "I need your permission to appoint a new interim sheriff."

The council members were old (average age sixty-three), and so there was not the melodramatic kind of rumbling you saw in bad movies. Instead there was a polite but prolonged silence as her words began to reverberate with implication.

"What's wrong with Sheriff Baines?" asked Samuel Coffey. He owned three DX stations and even though he'd never finished eighth grade was considered by many to be the brightest person on the council. "She's done a damn good job, far as I can tell."

Mrs. Kilrane said it quite simply. "Our esteemed sheriff, whom you profess to like so much, Mr. Coffey, is actually a common drug addict."

"What?"

"That's correct. I have learned on good authority—"

"Who's 'good authority'—"

"Someone quite reputable who wishes to remain anonymous for reasons that should be obvious." She lowered her voice and looked around the U. She was very good at this sort of thing. "We've all heard of 'rogue' law officers, people who take reprisals on honest citizens who turn them in."

This time it was Mr. Sale who spoke. Raymond Stockbridge had made Mr. Sale a millionaire several times over. You did not need to be a psychic to predict what the foolish man with wattles and a diamond stickpin was about to say.

"If Mrs. Kilrane and her father feel that the evidence is strong enough—" Mr. Sale began.

"What evidence?" Mr. Coffey demanded. His flat, fleshy face was clenched with anger. "This isn't evidence. This is nothing more than hearsay."

"But Mrs. Kilrane said—" sputtered Mr. Sale.

"I'm getting damn tired of being a rubber stamp for the Stockbridge family." Mr. Coffey glared at them. "And you fellows should be, too. God damnit, how about some integrity once in a while? That little gal's done a damn good job as sheriff and you know it. And she's no more a drug addict than I am."

He turned his anger on Mrs. Kilrane. "I can see what's happening here and I'm not going to stand for it. Sheriff Baines isn't going to get railroaded as long as I'm on this council, you can believe that."

Mrs. Kilrane looked to the back of the big room where a skinny young woman wearing a bulky sweater and jeans wrote furiously in a notepad. It was Connie Simmons, the new cub reporter from *Haversham Journal*. This was her first day on the City Hall beat. She couldn't have picked a more eventful one.

"I want to hear some more about this so-called

157

evidence," Mr. Coffey said. "And I'd also like to hear a little more about Gus Fenster's death last night. Our esteemed fire captain is saying that the man started a fire by smoking. But Gus was ordered by Doc Adams two months ago to give up the pipe." He narrowed his eyes. "So the smoking explanation seems very strange."

Instead of responding to Coffey's accusations, Mrs. Kilrane said, "I think we need a vote to see if we keep this meeting open."

The young reporter looked up from her notepad. "But these meetings have to be open. By law."

Mrs. Kilrane smiled. "Honey, why don't you go get yourself a cup of coffee at the sandwich stand downstairs. Put it on the council tab."

"But Mrs. Kilrane. By law—"

"Honey, don't make us go to the trouble of taking a vote. All right?"

Mr. Sale spoke up. "Young lady, I buy four full pages of advertising in your paper every week. I don't think your editor would like to hear that you'd displeased me."

Mr. Sale's point seemed to make glum sense to the young reporter. She rose, skinny except for a wide bottom, and fixed a pouty expression on her face.

"Mr. Adair wouldn't tolerate this at all," she said petulantly.

"Who," asked Mr. Sale, "is Mr. Adair?"

"My journalism instructor at State University."

"No," Mr. Sale smiled, "I don't suppose he would tolerate it. But that's why he lives in an ivory tower and we live in the real world."

A minute later the large doors leading to the

council chamber closed.

Mrs. Kilrane, angry as anybody could ever remember seeing her, jabbed a finger in Mr. Coffey's direction and said, "You ever embarrass me again like that, you sonofabitch, and you're through in Haversham. Do you understand me?"

Mayor Elliot Hughes sat in his office reading *USA Today*.

Mrs. Kilrane had told him she did not want him in the council meeting because of the way he sometimes vacillated on issues. She had expected trouble this morning, and when you expected trouble in Haversham, you did not want Elliot Hughes on your side.

So he sat reading his newspaper and eating his danish and sipping his coffee and thinking about the widow he used to work with at the hardware store. Tender images ignited his heart. Of all the women he'd known in his life, she'd had the least contempt for him.

His eyes fell on the phone.

Reach out and touch someone.

It would be so simple.

Sometimes he drove by her house. A light shone. He thought how wonderful it would be to sit in her parlor and watch her plump but beautiful body, dressed in something feminine and colorful, making him sweet treats with her hands, and later offering the sweetest treat of all, that rosebud between her legs that he had dreamed of for so long now, but had never had nerve to touch or taste, for fear of what his wife would do.

159

So simple to lift the receiver.

To call.

To arrange a meeting.

So simple.

He was in midreverie when his door was flung back.

There stood Mrs. Kilrane, wild-eyed behind the thickness of her glasses.

"Well, let's get Deputy Farnsworth and give him the news," she said.

"What news?" he asked, hurrying to put down his danish and his paper.

He always wanted to give people the impression he was busy, which was why he often carried a clipboard.

"The news that he's the acting sheriff."

"Then Diane Baines is—"

Mrs. Kilrane smiled and dragged a knifelike finger across her throat.

"Get your coat on, Mayor. We're going to pay a visit to her house."

His eyes fell again to the phone.

To the call he would probably never make now.

He rose from his mayoral chair, his perpetual frown tucked in the corner of his mouth.

"Do you really think we should do this?" he asked.

"You don't even have as many balls as my ex-husband," Mrs. Kilrane said. "And he only had half a one."

Mayor Hughes' secretary, who had made a minor art out of eavesdropping, burst out laughing.

By the time Diane Baines and John Tyler were on the road to the orphanage, the temperature had dropped another four degrees. Noontime in Haversham, despite the sunny day, was colder than early morning had been.

Tyler was enjoying himself. He hadn't felt this purposeful or sober in a long time. He looked out the car window at the ancient houses he'd played in or near as a boy. He had a sense of continuum, of being a part of some vast interconnection that some called the universe and others called God. He had good food in his belly and a new determination to stop his drinking. And he had a woman he was feeling a real hope about. With the two-way radio crackling and the sight of the small sirens on either fender, Tyler was taken back to his own days as sheriff. Good days they'd been, until he had cracked under the pressure of people kowtowing to the Stockbridge family. Oh, what vivid boozy fantasies he'd had back then— stalking into the city council chambers and confronting the weaklings who comprised that body, rubbing their faces in the truth of what their cowardice had wrought, not least of which was the murder of a small boy.

But that hadn't happened, of course.

Life wasn't like movies. In life you kept your

mouth shut and went on about your business until you couldn't take it anymore. Then you either moved on or you found some way of compensating for your grief and shame, which in his case meant alcohol and women.

"You sure look pensive," Diane smiled.

"Good word. That's exactly what I am. Pensive."

"Going to tell me what you're thinking about?"

So he did. At least partially. He couldn't get to all of it, no matter how much time he might have, no matter how articulate he might be. It was at such moments that Tyler always realized the inadequacy of words. How could you share with another human being the whole jumble of memories and sensory impressions that constituted a life? Your carpenter father whistling his way home, smelling of sawdust and pipe tobacco? The little nervous twitch in your mother's hand as she sat with her darning needle? The wan light in a sunset window as the lover you no longer cared about told you she was pregnant? These were the sights and sounds that only the grave knew and nurtured, those oddments of half-forgotten noises, odors, and expressions that were far more the essence of life than the big dramatic moments.

Time was all it was; time and the victims it made of everybody.

"Getting sentimental," he said.

"Tell me."

"Remembering my old man."

"What did he do?"

"Handyman. Worked for the sorghum plant until that shut down, then he worked for himself mostly. He always carried a green lunch bucket and swung it

162

in a wide arc as he walked. I can see him now." Tyler nodded to the sidewalk. A ghost appeared there—the old man himself, swinging his lunch pail, talking about how good Kramden and Norton would be this weekend on "The Jackie Gleason Show."

"You ever wish you could get in a time machine?" Tyler asked.

"Sure," she said. "If you find one, let me know. I'll be the first to buy a ticket."

He was about to say something when he saw the boy and girl dart out into the street in front of them.

In that terrible second he heard Diane scream as she expertly guided the car down the icy street so as to avoid the children.

"God," she said, "look!"

The boy had turned to face the men who pursued them, and he leveled his arm at them. The boy huddled into himself, as if he were having a seizure. The girl stood by him, sobbing and obviously terrified. The men moved in toward him. The boy's face came up from his hands—a contorted, insane face. His crazed eyes raised to a huge elm tree behind the men. The tree split in half in a jagged bolt of flame. Venerable wood cracked like a tooth being ripped out by a sadistic dentist.

A huge branch fell on one of the men. Screaming, he was crushed to the ground.

Ten minutes earlier, after watching Brian and Caroline sneak down the stairs, Mr. Rydell had gone to find Ken Dodge, Windhaven's PE instructor and the man everybody feared second only to Mrs.

163

Kilrane herself.

Mr. Rydell disliked Ken Dodge a great deal and with good reason.

At a faculty mixer, shortly after Mr. Rydell had come to Windhaven, Ken Dodge had put his hand on his hip and minced around after Mr. Rydell all night, implying that this was how Mr. Rydell walked, implying all sorts of things about Mr. Rydell. People ssshed Dodge, people scolded him, but this had only seemed to egg him on, to make him even meaner. Only the eventual presence of Mrs. Kilrane had checked Dodge. She did not like arguments among staff members—if there were to be any, she would be their source.

All these memories troubled Mr. Rydell—wouldn't it be nice to have no memory at all, simply to float on momentary sensation (nice smells, nice textures, nice daydreams)?—as he approached the gym where Ken Dodge daily beat and pounded his body into almost useless perfection. He was too old for Mr. America and too young to be a phenomenon à la Jack LaLane, so what was the point?

Mr. Rydell wouldn't have gone to Ken Dodge in the first place, except that he knew that Mrs. Kilrane was in town, which meant that Dodge was in charge.

"Hi, sweets," Dodge said from the parallel bars when Mr. Rydell walked into the gym.

The floors were covered with tumbling mats. Bleachers sat empty, like jilted lovers.

"I've asked you," Mr. Rydell said, "not to call me that."

"Gee," Dodge said. "I sure don't want to make you mad."

"You're not very funny."

"Well you are, honey. You're very funny."

Mr. Rydell had had long practice at being treated like a freak. After a time you even developed scar tissue. "Two of our students are running away."

Dodge was like a pointer dog.

At Mr. Rydell's words, he jumped down from the parallel bars. He hit the wooden floor like an explosion.

"Where are they?"

Mr. Rydell told him.

Dodge pushed past him, nearly knocking him down.

When the tree limb hit Mr. Rydell, part of his brains came out through his nose and part of them through his ears.

In that instant Ken Dodge had a sense of total unreality, as if he were trapped in a nightmare that was both serious and comic.

Here (the real part) you had a very real cold midwestern winter morning—sun out, frost shining on car windows and car hoods, trucks swishing sand on icy roads, babies walking around in snowsuits, bulky as moon people—and then . . .

And then (the unreal part) you were walking across the street and the g.d. tree splits in half and falls on that g.d. faggot Mr. Rydell, squishing his brains out of him like so much catsup in a g.d. squeeze tube.

And all the time this kid, Brian Courtney, is carrying on as if he was possessed by g.d. demons or something.

Dodge looked down at Rydell, whose eyes were oozing squishy stuff now, then looked up to see the sheriff's car skidding icily into the curb.

Diane Baines was out of the car before it came to a complete halt.

In her confusion and bewilderment, she unflapped her holster. But she knew already that her Smith and Wesson would be no help against the disaster that had occurred.

Moments later, John Tyler caught up with her. They edged toward the two children.

"Stay away!" cried the girl.

From a hundred yards away, Diane could see that the pretty child was as frightened and perplexed as Diane herself. Obviously the girl was trying to help the young boy—who had fallen on the ground, clutching his head as if in response to a tumor, screaming in agony. Diane had never seen a headache affect anyone this way. Her impression was that he was having some kind of epileptic seizure.

Diane pressed forward.

"Stay away!" cried the girl again.

But in the crisp midday air, onlookers beginning to stream from nearby houses, Diane and Tyler continued to move in on their prey.

Dodge remained unmoving.

Frozen.

Near his feet, Mr. Rydell had begun to twitch in his final moments of life.

"We're not going to hurt you," Diane said to the girl. True to the training she'd received in various police departments, she spoke slowly and gently. You needed to convince people like the little boy that you were on his side.

The boy still seemed to be in his stupor. With his tousled hair and cute little face, it was easy to forget for a moment what had happened a few minutes earlier.

But there was a terrible reminder of the boy's strange powers in the person of the man dying so terribly in the street.

"Easy," John Tyler said. "Careful." His voice was scarcely a whisper as he moved in unison with Diane.

Suddenly the boy shot up.

"No!" the girl cried, throwing her arms toward the boy.

But the boy's face already showed unmistakable signs of rage—the same signs that had preceded his explosion earlier.

He got to his feet.

Obviously his headache was still with him, because his eyes squinted and he had to slam a small hand against his temple.

"Be careful!" Diane shouted to Tyler.

Tyler seemed to be moving too quickly toward the boy.

Tyler nodded.

The boy turned quickly—as if he were blind, as if he had no control over himself—toward the street, where a new Chevrolet was parked.

The car exploded, turning in a single moment into a tumbling orange ball of flame.

The onlookers screamed and ran for shelter from the flying debris.

Diane and Tyler started moving for the boy again, but he surprised them by ripping away from the girl and heading in the direction of the swampy area.

"Brian!" the little girl cried.

But he didn't stop.

He ran past the onlookers, up the frozen grassy hill and under the fence that surrounded the swampy area.

The little girl fell into Diane's waiting embrace, sobbing, her frail body feeling as though it were on fire.

"Go after him," Diane said to Tyler.

Brian did not know what was happening to him—he ran, his lungs afire, his brain a jumble of images, needs and fears—as behind him the shouts of people who hated him could be heard even above his hammering heart.

Tyler parted the strands of fencing just as he saw the little boy run to the edge of the swamp.

He saw instantly what the kid was going to do.

"Don't!" Tyler screamed.

But already it was too late.

With his heel, the kid was digging in the ice, creating a hole big enough to slip through.

Tyler cut his hand on the fencing, tearing a deep red gash in his palm.

But he knew there was no time to slow down.

He ran over to the kid, still yelling for him to stop, but it was too late.

The kid glanced back only once.

Then he jumped in.

He disappeared as if he'd been dropped down a shaft.

Tyler, panting, his hand running from blood, threw himself beside the hole the kid had opened up.

Filthy, chemically polluted water was all that could be seen.

Below, somewhere in the murk, they would find the body of the kid.

Floating.

Part Two

Chapter Eight

1

The hearing was held four days later, in a large courtroom next to the city council chambers.

Present were the entire council, including the mayor, and the Stockbridge family, including Raymond Stockbridge and Mrs. Kilrane. Gray midmorning light pressed against the windows. Heat clanged through the steam pipes.

The proceedings had been going on for the past half-hour. The focus of those proceedings sat in a chair facing the long table of questioners. Diane wore her uniform out of obstinacy. She fully expected that she would be let go because of the trumped-up drug charges, but she hoped her uniform would remind at least a few of them that she had served the town well.

Raymond Stockbridge held up a plastic bag containing white powder. It was tagged much the way a piece of evidence would be at a criminal trial.

"Do you deny, Miss Baines, that you kept this in your home?"

He played his usual self-righteous self this morning. She had to admit he was good at it. She could easily see him as Henry VIII, dispatching anybody who pleased him.

"Yes, I do deny it," she said.

Raymond Stockbridge frowned and pursed his lips. "Why don't we all be nice to each other, Miss Baines, and get this over with. We don't plan to press criminal charges against you. We'd just like you to admit your wrongdoing and then leave Haversham."

Diane allowed a bitchy smirk to part her lips. "Wouldn't that be convenient for you?"

"And just what is that supposed to mean?" Stockbridge asked.

She addressed the council. "It means that you drummed up the drug charges because you knew that I was going to investigate the death of David Mason."

"That's ridiculous," Stockbridge said.

"There's also the matter of another small boy who died fifteen years ago. Supposedly in a hit-and-run that was never solved." She glared at him. "But there is evidence that points to the fact that the car that struck the boy came from Windhaven. I believe you own Windhaven, don't you, Mr. Stockbridge?"

She could see him visibly shrink from her accusation.

She was about to press him further when something slammed the table to her left.

A riding crop.

Mrs. Kilrane, looking almost pretty in a white

174

turtleneck sweater and a tan suede car coat, brought her riding crop down against the edge of the table.

"I'm not going to see my father humiliated any more! And you men should be ashamed of yourselves for letting her speak to him this way."

She got the response she wanted.

Mr. Sale, ever eager to please the family that had made him a millionaire, sat up rigidly in his chair and said, "We're not giving you your choice in this matter, Miss Baines. We're firing you right here and now and ordering you to leave town."

"I would like to know who found the cocaine in my place and on what authority you entered my house?"

Mr. Sale looked uncomfortable. "You're forcing us to do something we'd rather not, Miss Baines."

"I have a right to know."

Mrs. Kilrane and Mr. Sale exchanged an obscure expression. Then Mr. Sale nodded to a bailiff who stood by the two large oak doors that led into the room.

The bailiff opened one of the doors and a man in a uniform came in. A tall man, slightly disheveled in the way Fred MacMurray was always disheveled.

His familiar grin and flirty expression were gone. He looked grim enough to be attending the funeral of a close friend. He came into the room and stood over by the table where the council sat, as if they were going to protect him.

Then Diane noticed something new about him.

The badge on his chest was no longer the round deputy's badge. Bill Farnsworth now wore the four-pointed star of the sheriff.

Apparently Raymond Stockbridge kept several of the things on hand, in case he needed to hand them out.

But her anger waned even before he spoke. Instead she felt an oppressive sense of betrayal. In that instant she felt as if she were mad—the world was an unknowable and unfathomable place. Nobody was who or what they seemed.

"I believe you know this man, Mr. Farnsworth," Raymond Stockbridge said.

So Bill Farnsworth was to be their Judas Goat. The man would testify against her. Bill Farnsworth, the man she'd considered going out with, even sleeping with.

"Yes," she said, depression already giving her voice a dull edge. "Yes, I know this man."

The rest of the hearing took less than ten minutes. Bill Farnsworth didn't once meet her eye.

"You going to let me say anything?"

"No."

"I'd like to explain."

"There's nothing to say."

"I—they—well, they forced me to say what I did."

She stopped. Turned and faced him there in the parking lot of the courthouse.

"I'm surprised you even want to be seen speaking to me," she said. She wanted to cry, but she was damned if she would give him the satisfaction.

"Two children have died at Windhaven," she said. "I think Stockbridge somehow had something to do with it. But you and the rest of the city council are covering up for him."

With that she turned around again and stalked to her car.

He trailed along behind her, whipped and embarrassed.

He stood by her car—helplessly—as she opened the door.

"Diane, I love you."

She only shook her head. "You've got great timing, Farnsworth. Great timing."

Then she got in, slammed the door, and drove off.

The girl was waiting for Diane on the front steps of the small house she would now have to put up for sale.

She didn't look up while Diane parked the car in the driveway, nor did she look up when Diane walked over to her. Even from a distance you could see the kid had been sitting there a long time. Her nose and cheeks were red from the cold, overcast morning. Her lips were a bloodless white.

The house in the bleak weather had a shabby, depressing aspect. The dead grass was brown and the white shingles looked in need of serious washing. Diane just wanted to go in, fix herself her father's remedy of coffee with bourbon in it, then spend the rest of the afternoon in the bathtub, luxuriating in sudsy water and self-pity.

"Hello, Caroline," Diane said.

Caroline Hayes was an exceptionally pretty girl, with the cheekbones and forehead of a model. Her blond hair hung in pigtails. The spray of freckles across her face only made her more appealing.

"You look like you could use some hot chocolate," Diane said.

So much for the hot bath idea.

But actually she felt grateful for the distraction from her own misery.

"Come on," Diane said, holding out her hand.

Caroline didn't take it.

She just looked up at her with a clear blue expression that conveyed both intelligence and heartbreak.

"I ran away," she said.

Diane, seeing that Caroline was long past even noticing the cold, decided to sit down next to her.

They sat next to each other on the porch without speaking for a time. Cars went by. In the small house across the street Christmas lights twinkled on and off. The old woman who lived there was obviously comforted by the lights. Given her existence on Social Security, such an indulgence required a budget sacrifice somewhere. Diane hoped she had enough to eat.

"I don't think he's dead," Caroline said.

"Who?"

"Brian."

Diane kept her voice cool. "Why do you say that?"

Caroline shrugged. "I'm not sure."

After Brian had run to the swampy area and thrown himself in, Diane had stayed with the bereaved little girl for the next four hours. They had gotten to be friends. And now Caroline's assertion that Brian might be alive was very troubling. Perhaps the shock of the incident . . .

Diane reached over and slid her arm around Caroline.

"If I ever have a daughter, I hope she's just like you."

"You don't believe me, do you?"

"Honey, listen, we searched for Brian for several

179

hours. I don't think—"

"You remember what he did with that energy beam, don't you?"

"Well, yes, honey but—"

This time Diane stopped herself.

When the subject of what had emitted from Brian's finger came up, there was very little she had to say.

John Tyler and she had spent most of the night sitting across her kitchen table trying to convince themselves that what they'd seen had somehow been a terrible coincidence.

The tree had just happened to come apart just then—"

The blue arc of energy was some kind of mass hallucination combined with subtle atmospheric changes—

"I ran away," Caroline said. "I figured since you were the sheriff, you could help me."

"I'm afraid I've got some bad news for you, honey. I'm not the sheriff anymore."

She felt Caroline stiffen under her arm.

"Why not?"

Diane explained.

"They're guilty, aren't they? Everybody who works at the orphanage. Everybody on the city council. They know what really happened to Davie Mason. And they won't tell the truth about it."

"I'm afraid that's the way it looks."

Caroline reached in her pocket. "I think they were going to do something to Brain, too."

She showed Diane a well-crafted toy soldier.

Diane fumbled with it between her gloved fingers. "Where did you get this?"

"Brian gave it to me."

"Brian?"

Caroline nodded solemnly. "He said that Mr. Stockbridge gave it to him right after he hit him on the hand."

Caroline went on to relate all the things Brian had told her. About Raymond Stockbridge's warning of something terrible happening if Brain didn't tell the truth within forty-eight hours. About finding Davie Mason's things, including an identical toy soldier, up under the mattress—and then everything being taken away, so no evidence was left. And then about Davie's voice from the swampy area.

When she finished, Caroline slumped inside her bulky winter coat.

"Pepsi, huh?"

"Yeah. Pepsi."

During some of his worst binges, Tyler had sometimes ended up here, at the Eight Ball Tavern, one of those places where the jukebox glass was always shattered from a fistfight a few night ago, and where the urinals were rarely usable because of people puking in them. Tyler had come here because he had remembered something about Mrs. Kilrane's husband. The guy's uncle was the owner of this dump.

The time was midafternoon. Willie Nelson sang of melancholy days, the bumper pool game went on with the intensity of an Olympic event, and the bartender spent most of his time trying to secretly pick his nose.

Tyler, chill from the cold, wrapped his hand around the Pepsi and let the stuff cut through the dryness of his throat.

Despite all the things that had happened over the past four days, despite even the fact that Diane had lost her job, there was no denying the good feeling Tyler was getting from tracking down some facts.

He was a born cop and it was good to be in harness again.

"Owner around?" Tyler asked the bartender.

"Merle?"

"If he's the owner."

"Why?"

"Need to speak to him."

"You're Tyler, right?"

"Right."

"Used to be sheriff?"

Tyler nodded.

"Used to be don't cut shit. Not in this place, anyway."

A toothless old man along the bar smiled his terrible smile.

"Need to see Merle," Tyler said. "Now."

He tried hard to sound self-confident. But the years of being naked of the badge, the years of drinking away his days, had left him without the emotional reserves for a small crisis like this.

The bartender, a fleshy man with greasy gray hair, only sneered. "You want to see Merle, you better call him first and set up an appointment."

The old man put down his *Enquirer* and started paying attention to the scene at the bar. This was even more exciting than the sex secrets of the stars.

Behind the bar, the phone rang.

The bartender reached down to grab it and when he did, Tyler made his move. There was a door that Tyler vaguely remembered led upstairs. He ran to it, jerked it open, found himself facing a sheer flight of steps. As the door banged shut behind him, he heard the bartender start to yell.

Tyler took the steps two at a time. Dust and grime coated the walls on either side of the narrow staircase. When he got to the top he found himself in a room that vaguely resembled a living room. Facing him was a huge man in biker getup. A leather vest tried but failed to cover a stomach the size of a small Latin American country, and a leather band tied together filthy wild hair. The guy wore an eyepatch. He also leveled a Remington double-barreled shotgun at Tyler.

"Shit, Tyler," the guy grinned. "For a punk like you, I sure don't need this."

He set down the shotgun. From his belt he took a Bowie knife. Placed it carefully on his lap.

"This'll do fine," the guy smiled.

He was in his fifties and had enough scar tissue on his face and arms to do a whole regiment of combat veterans proud.

All Tyler could do was stand there and gape.

"You don't remember me, do you?" the guy smiled unpleasantly.

"Afraid I don't."

"You run me in one night." He snorted. "You and three other cops. Took four of you candy-asses."

Tyler looked more carefully.

Nothing.

"'Course I put on a few pounds since then." The guy broke up. He seemed to find all this very funny. "'Bout two hunnerd, I reckon."

"Are you Merle?"

"You got that right, Tyler."

"You were Bob Kilrane's uncle?"

Merle's face got taut. "You damn right I was."

"You don't like me very much. I wonder why," Tyler said.

Merle rubbed the shotgun again. "You know

damn well why, Tyler. Don't try to shit me."

Tyler stood his ground.

"I don't know what you're talking about," he said.

"You and your bosses, the Stockbridges. Ask them."

"About what?"

"About what they did with the body. They killed little Bobby and buried him somewhere. As if you didn't already fuckin' know."

Tyler decided to give the man time to cool down a bit.

He looked around the shabby room. Orange crates were filled with records. Several Waylon Jennings posters covered one wall, Sylvester Stallone posters another. There was a litter box for cats. It probably hadn't been emptied, at least from the smell of it, in a year or two.

When he looked back, Tyler found himself staring at the shotgun again.

"Just what the hell are you doin' here, anyway, Tyler?"

"Looking for some help."

"What kind of help?"

"Help in getting the Stockbridges."

Merle studied him. "No bullshit?"

"No bullshit."

Merle stood up.

The floor creaked.

He was taller and wider than Tyler. He was also about three times deadlier.

He wore an earring in one ear and a soiled bandana around his neck.

He went over to a lopsided kitchen table and

snatched up a bottle of Thunderbird. "I don't suppose you'd care for any."

"Not right now."

"You give it up? The nights you came in here, you sure didn't look like the kind who'd ever do a fool thing like that." The snottiness was back in his voice.

"You going to help me?"

"Yeah, Sheriff, you fucking right I'm going to help you."

And with that, the huge man whirled around like a big piece of machinery that had been ripped from its moorings.

The first thing he caught Tyler with was a solid blow to the stomach.

Next came a knee to the groin.

Then came a straight hard shot to the jaw, delivered with surprising grace and unbelievable force.

Tyler tried to gather enough strength to throw his own punch, but he felt himself being slammed against the wall and knew that self-defense at this point would be impossible.

The biker had two things going—rage and overwhelming strength.

Merle put his battered face into Tyler's and screamed, "Now you get outta here, you understand! I don't want no Stockbridge flunky sniffin' around me!"

To prove his point, he lifted Tyler even higher, pounding the back of Tyler's skull against the wall.

Merle ended the encounter by dragging Tyler over to the stairs and throwing him down.

Fortunately, Tyler got some leverage on the

narrow steps and stopped himself from tumbling all the way down.

As he entered the tavern, all eyes following his passage, he saw the bartender smile at the toothless old man.

They were happy as hell.

Tyler left.

4

In the dream, he called to her.

In the dream, he stood next to the bed where she slept and put out a hand.

In the dream, they ran away together, away from everything the Stockbridge family had ever touched.

In the dream they were safe and warm and happy.

When she woke, trying desperately to cling to the stray fragments of the dream, Caroline knew instantly that the world was not the happy place her subconscious mind had conjured up.

Brain was dead. He was not calling out to her, and he was not standing by her bed.

Her tears came easily.

"Caroline."

In the windy late afternoon, Diane's voice was almost lost.

The former sheriff, now in a blue crew neck sweater and jeans instead of her uniform, stood in the doorway with a tray.

Even from where she lay Caroline could smell the buttery toast and hot chocolate.

She had not slept well since Brian had killed himself.

She liked it here, liked Diane especially, and that helped her appetite.

Diane came in and sat next to her on the bed.

"Caroline, I think maybe it's time we call the orphanage," she said gently.

Caroline's appetite disappeared again.

All she could think of was Mrs. Kilrane and her fury and cruelty. And her smug smile now that Brian was dead—and Caroline was more isolated than ever.

"It won't be so bad," Diane said. "In a few days your new adoptive parents will take you and—"

Caroline frowned. She had yet to tell Diane the news. "Mrs. Kilrane called them yesterday. They seem to be having second thoughts."

Diane's face tightened in the dying light of the bedroom. With its small canopy bed, neatly arranged dressing table, and its array of stuffed animals, the bedroom suggested a woman who still had a strong streak of little girl.

"So they're not going to take you?"

"That's what Mrs. Kilrane says."

"I see."

Diane's voice was tight, cold, as if she were afraid to express her real feelings.

Then Diane smiled down at the tray on the bed. "Why don't you eat the toast, honey, before it gets cold?"

Caroline shrugged. Food sounded like a good idea. "All right."

Diane leaned over and hugged her. "Don't worry. Things will work out."

"Do we have to call Windhaven?"

Diane's answer surprised and pleased Caroline. "No. Not right now."

Diane stood up. "Now go ahead and eat. I—I've got things I should do around the house. Maybe you'll feel like having another small nap."

Caroline yawned, as if on cue.

She was still tired. The days since Brian's death had exhausted her.

"See you in a while," Diane said.

Fifteen minutes later, Caroline slipped into a deep sleep.

Her first dream was a fantasy. All the stuffed animals in the bedroom suddenly came alive and formed a dancing circle. Caroline joined them in their dance. It was fun, a lot of fun.

But then the voice started.

Caroline.

Even asleep, a part of her mind knew this was real.

Caroline.

At first she was not sure who was calling her. Only gradually, as the dream of the dancing animals went on, did she begin to recognize the voice.

When she came awake this time it was dark. A muzzy streetlight played against the window, a blowing tree branch making jerky patterns on the light. Caroline was chill with sweat, as if she were coming down with something.

Caroline.

There was a certain time of day when Mrs. Kilrane got sentimental.

Had the people around her, the people forced to suffer her ego, her temper, her madness—had they been told she was sentimental this way, they would have laughed off the idea.

She locked herself in the den, the fireplace roaring, and put a special record on the stereo.

Bobby Vinton singing "Blue on Blue."

She sat in the big leather chair where her father the patriarch sometimes sat, rolled expensive wine around in an expensive goblet, and stared at the fireplace as if it were dancing with images to be studied, the way a movie screen might.

She saw herself and her young husband dancing to the Bobby Vinton song.

For her twenty-fourth birthday he'd bought her a wrist corsage, an extravagant purple flower, which she'd worn to the steak house where they'd had dinner.

Oh, she was well aware that people snickered at her behind her back. How could a tomboy like her enjoy anything as feminine as a flower? they asked each other sarcastically. But it wasn't her fault that she'd been born as much man as woman—and it didn't make her a damn bit less feminine, either.

The fire . . .

Then the sentimental moment was spoiled when she thought of that rainy Friday night when she'd found the pretty schoolteacher here at Windhaven and her husband together in the pantry—

Her eyes raised toward the ceiling. To the attic.

Where her husband presently resided.

Where he would reside for all eternity.

A rage seized her. The same rage that had overwhelmed her the moment she'd walked in on—

The phone rang, interrupting her building anger.

"Yes?" she snapped.

"This is Sale," said the voice.

Sale. The city council flunky who had worked for the Stockbridge family for so many years.

"Yes?" Her harsh tone had not changed.

"I thought I'd pass along some information."

"About what?"

"About Coffey."

"What about him, Mr. Sale?"

"He, uh, well he's none too happy that we fired the sheriff. He likes her."

"Mr. Coffey's likes and dislikes don't concern me, Mr. Sale."

"I think he's going to consult a lawyer."

"Let him."

Mr. Sale suddenly got very defensive. Obviously he'd expected Mrs. Kilrane to thank him cordially.

She had no such plans.

"Is that all?"

"Uh, well, yes, I guess it is."

"Then good night, Mr. Sale."

"But Mrs. Kilrane, I don't think you're—" He

paused. "You never can tell what Coffey will do. That's what makes him dangerous. Ask your father."

My father, she thought angrily. Then she thought of where the old man was right now. The most powerful man in Haversham.

She had to smile. Then she said, "Good night, Mr. Sale."

She hung up, went back to her leather seat by the fire. She picked up her wine, smelled it, tasted it. The smile came back to her lips as her gaze rose to the attic above her.

Sometimes he worried about fire—if a fire happened up here, he would die for sure—but he supposed that as angry as she got with him, she would make sure that he was rescued.

She had gotten the idea from her mother.

His wife used to send him up here, too. Lock the stairway door on him.

But at least in those days there hadn't been a—

Raymond Stockbridge's eyes searched the darkness for the outline of the urn.

In the darkness, Stockbridge imagined he could see eyes, eyes that scorned him just as his own daughter's did.

In the darkness, the eyes kept staring at him.

6

A year ago reality had forced Coffey to convert his main DX station into one of those modern convenience stores that only incidentally sold gas.

You could get Hostess Twinkies, you could get Winston cigarettes, you could get Fenro combs . . . you could get everything up to and including Trojans.

Which was a hell of a way for a man who made his living as an A-1 mechanic to make a living.

Now he stood on the drive, glad to be pumping Mrs. Chandler's gas. It was one of the few remaining duties that still reminded him of the old days when Coffey and his crew hit the drive to wash windows, fill tires, pump gas, and check oil. These days most people wanted to do many if not most of those things themselves.

Full night had descended on Haversham now. A frosty moon rode the sky. Smoke snaked grayly up from chimneys. Cars went by chinking with tire chains. The weathermen were warning about a winter storm in less than forty-eight hours.

Coffey stood on the drive, enjoying the smells of gas, oil, and a warm car engine. These were the smells of his life. His old man had owned a City Service station. Coffey had grown up working in it. He wanted to be doing the same kind of work when his turn came to die.

The pump shut off. Mrs. Chandler's car was full. He went inside, wrote up her ticket. The two younger men had changed the station back to rock and roll, which irritated Coffey. He liked the station that played the oldies, Vic Damone and Nat "King" Cole. People who could really sing.

On his way out to the drive, he glanced at the phone.

He wondered if he were really going to do it. He had never considered himself a brave man. During World War II he had spent nineteen months so scared that he had been constipated for weeks at a time.

So what he had in mind now . . .

He gave Mrs. Chandler her change and went back into the station.

He had planned to start gabbing with one of the young guys, hoping their conversation would dissuade him from picking up the phone and—

But both the kids were busy. One with a flat tire. The other filling the bread racks. (Bread racks—now there was something you never saw in his old man's City Service station. You bought bread in a frigging bakery, back in those days, not in a frigging gas station.)

Nor were there any customers to distract him.

So all there was to do for the next few minutes was stare at the phone as if he were trying to levitate the thing, stare at it and consider the implications of the action he was thinking about taking. . . .

"You wanna take a break, Mel?" Coffey asked the sandy-haired young man.

"Nah, I better keep working, Mr. Coffey. We need

some more Ding-Dongs put out."

Ding-Dongs!

Did the young kid realize how stupid that sounded coming from somebody who should have been fixing motors instead of loading sugary goodies onto racks?

"Ah, come on," Coffey said.

He eyed the phone like an alcoholic eyeing a drink. Scared.

"Nah, really, Mr. Coffey, I really better keep working here."

"Shit," Coffey said under his breath.

He knew in that instant he was going to do it.

Pick up the phone.

Make the call.

And perhaps destroy his life here in Haversham.

Chapter Nine

1

"I can't think of a better excuse for a drink," Tyler told Diane after she plunked him into a straight-backed kitchen chair and began applying first aid to his various cuts and bruises.

"Neither can I," she said seriously.

"But I think I'll resist and settle for a nice cold Pepsi when you get done here."

She hugged him. She was getting back into that habit again—being physical with people she cared about—first Caroline this afternoon—and now Tyler. It felt great.

Tyler had told her all about his visit with Merle the biker.

So she asked again, daubing iodine on his chin, "I guess I still don't understand how he could help us."

"If we can't force the Stockbridges' hand on their involvement in the death of the children, maybe we can prove that Mrs. Kilrane had something to do with the disappearance of her husband."

"Hard to believe she was ever married."

He smiled grimly. "I guess I wouldn't ever ask her to dance, now that you put it that way."

She shook her head. "I wasn't being unkind about her looks. I mean—I just sense this great turmoil inside her—this rage, but at the same time this loneliness. I don't think she cares for her father a great deal."

"Really? That surprises me."

"I sense she's his keeper—probably even his boss—but I think she finds him vaguely distasteful. Though I'm not sure why."

"Hey!" He half laughed and half winced. "You would have made a great Dr. Frankenstein."

She had just sprayed some Bactine on a cut. "He must have been wearing rings."

"He was," Tyler said, "but given the size of his hands and the power of his swing, I think he could have done just fine bare-knuckled."

"Wasn't worth it, I guess, your visit."

"No. For some reason, he thinks I'm still in thick with the Stockbridges."

"That's a reasonable assumption in this town. You never know who's on your side and who's not."

He looked at her levelly. "Still bothers you, doesn't it?"

"What?"

"Your deputy. Farnsworth. Selling you out that way."

"Yes, I guess it does."

He took her arm and sat her on his lap.

There was wind rattling the window. A wintry night sky painted the panes black. Yet in his embrace she felt warm, needed, safe.

Which was when, of course, the phone rang.

She might have thought of letting it ring on and on till the caller hung up—but something in the tone of the ringing seemed urgent.

She got up to get it.

"Damn," she said.

He grinned. "Double damn for me."

In the bedroom the sound of the ringing phone roused Caroline.

She woke again to find sweat covering her body, as if a fever had claimed her.

Caroline.

She knew the voice was in her mind, yet it seemed to fill this whole room, this whole house.

Caroline.

Brian, of course.

Calling her.

Summoning her.

To join him.

She did not have to ask where.

Or why.

By now it was very clear to her.

"Hello," Diane said.

The voice was instantly recognizable.

Lou Coffey had a voice that was a testament to what cigarettes did to the vocal chords. It was like listening to a buzz saw trying to cut steel.

"Wondered if you could meet me a little later," he said.

She had always liked Coffey. At council meetings he was the only one with courage enough to oppose the Stockbridge flunkies. But now, after her experience with Farnsworth, she wondered if she could trust Coffey. Earlier that night—a wave of paranoia washing over her—she had wondered if she could even trust John Tyler. He might be a plant, a sort of double agent, for the Stockbridge family, pretending to be an outcast, while in reality being—

"Yes," she said, forcing herself back to reality. She had to trust somebody. Otherwise, she would go insane.

"All right. Where would you like to meet?"

"You know where the Dekker farm is?"

Again alarm bells sounded: Why would he want to meet at a deserted farmhouse far from town?

"Why there?" she said. The edge in her voice made it obvious she was nervous.

"Something I want to show you."

She tried to interject some humor. "Don't I get a sneak preview?"

"I'll just see you there. Around ten o'clock?"

"Fine."

Coffey hung up.

When she turned back to the kitchen table, she saw Tyler sitting there.

In his hand he fiddled with a toy soldier. The one Caroline had held.

He seemed astonished. "Where did you get this?" he asked.

"From Caroline. Stockbridge had given it to Brian. And to Davie Mason."

He looked at her earnestly. "Fifteen years ago, the little boy who was killed in the hit-and-run?"

She nodded.

"I found a toy soldier identical to this one in his pocket."

2

"Finish your spinach."

"But I don't like spinach."

She smiled. "Now you go ahead and finish it. Isn't that right?"

"That's right," said Biff.

"That's right," said Buffy.

So Mayor Elliot Hughes went ahead and finished his spinach with his wife and children beaming at him proudly, the way they always beamed at him proudly whenever he did what they wanted him to.

"I'm told there's a new sheriff," said Mrs. Mayor as Mr. Mayor finished the last strandy bits of the green stuff.

"Ummmrrgmmm," said the mayor, chewing.

"Well, I'm glad of that," Mrs. Mayor said with a decisive cluck of the tongue. "That was no job for a woman."

The mayor knew enough to nod in agreement. If he hadn't, there would have been hell to pay.

"Look at that plate," marveled Mrs. Mayor when Mr. Mayor was finished.

She reached over and picked it up, considering the little bits of spinach that clung to it. She held it up to the light as if it were precious gold shining in sunlight.

"Just look at that plate," she sang. "So clean and

all-gone. Isn't that wonderful, children?"

"Well," the mayor said, standing up and patting at his paunch. He was a rail-thin man who'd always wanted a paunch, one of the comfortable kind that looked good in bib overalls and being patted by a big masculine hand. "Guess I'd better be heading back to the office."

Mrs. Mayor looked horrified. "The office? Why, dear, are you forgetting that Pat Robertson's guest on the 800 Club is Pat Boone?"

"No," said the mayor, "no, I'm not forgetting."

"Then why would you go back to the office?"

"Well, Farnsworth, the man we made sheriff, he thinks he needs some help and—"

Mrs. Mayor seemed unable to resist. In her tartest voice, she said, "So, he's turning to a big manly man like yourself to teach him all about law and order?"

For once, the mayor didn't let her sarcasm slide. In a steady voice, he said, "You haven't given me much opportunity lately to prove if I'm a man or not."

Mrs. Mayor looked scandalized.

She reached over and clamped her hands firmly on Buffy's ears.

Before she could say anything, the mayor himself had gone out the back door, grabbing his heavy winter coat on the way.

Yellow headlights splashed against the garage. Then the sound of a transmission whining in reverse.

The mayor was gone.

He hadn't even asked permission.

"Hello, Emma?"

"This is Emma."

"This is El."

She'd never called him Elliot. Always El. Said it was shorter.

"El. My God! El. Is it really you?"

"It's really me."

"Well, how are you?"

She conveyed a genuinely happy feeling.

He forgot he was standing in a bleak, battered phone booth covered with graffiti and smelling of piss. He forgot the wind that rattled the booth and the cows that mooed in the darkness somewhere on a nearby hill. Instead her voice evoked memories of different times—of the bright cake she'd baked for one of his birthdays, of the way he'd held her after the news of her husband's auto accident, the day at the library when she'd shown him a shot of herself in a thirty-year-old newspaper—six she'd been, in a spangly little baton twirler's costume. The sweetness of that moment had never left him—he'd felt privy to the greatest secret two people had ever shared.

"How have you been?" she asked.

"Oh, fine."

"Must be something, being mayor and all. I always tell people I used to know you. They seem impressed. They really do."

"Well, Haversham isn't really that big a—"

"I saw you on the street once and I almost stopped you."

"Oh, you should have, Emma. You should have." There was real yearning in his voice, warm as the night was cold.

"But now that you're mayor— Well, people

change with positions, El. You know that."

There were the words on his lips—the words he'd dreaded and revered for so many years—*I love you.*

"So how are your children?" she said.

"Good. Real good."

"They must be getting old now."

"Six and eight."

"Six and eight! Why just yesterday—"

I love you, Emma.

Then a silence ensued and they just listened to the electronic buzzing in the lines, the shifts in patterns of phone communications.

"Emma," he said finally.

"Yes?"

"I—I've missed you."

"Oh," she said. "I don't think you should say that, El. Being married and all."

"But I have."

"Well."

"And I'd like to come see you."

Silence again.

"Emma?"

"Please, El. Don't say anything just now."

"All right."

So the electronic silence ensued again.

Then Emma said, "You remember that day I baked a birthday cake for you?"

"I sure do."

"Well, I gave you the cake and I gave you the necktie, but I didn't give you the letter."

"Letter?"

"Yes. I'd written you a letter while the cake was baking."

"I didn't see any letter."

"I know." She paused. "I burned it."

"Burned it? Why would you do that?"

"Because it expressed my true feelings and because my true feelings didn't have any right to be expressed, you being a married man, with a wife and two children, with a responsible job in the community and president of Lions."

"Oh, Emma."

He had not felt this thrilled since he'd been a teenager.

"I want to hang up now."

"Please, don't Emma."

"Good-bye, El."

Click.

The conversation was over.

Ten minutes later, Elliot Hughes pulled his big Buick up to the curb.

Before him lay Emma's house.

In all the years he'd known her, he'd never had nerve enough to come over here, even though in his dreams he'd visited it many times.

He got out of the car, letting the raw cold of the night revive his skin, sluggish from the car heater.

The bungalow looked tidy and clean in the darkness. A yellow light glowed behind two screened windows. A walk, already dusted with snow, went straight from the curb to the front door.

Then something startling and wonderful happened.

The front door was flung open and there stood Emma.

"I'm so glad you came, El! I'm so glad you came!"

By the time he touched her—his arms feeling as if they were embracing the one person God had meant for him to embrace—he was already crying with joy.

She led him inside then, to the house he'd always dreamed of, the evening he'd always planned.

With its fireplace, its built-in bookshelves, its softly glowing TV, the room could not have seemed more inviting. He had even ceased worrying about what would happen if some citizen saw him coming in here.

Let them talk.

He took her in his arms and kissed her.

3

When he was finished, Doc Adams shut off the microscope, wiped his brow free from sweat, and left the small laboratory the state provided its coroners.

The morgue was chill and empty as he passed through it. The drawers containing bodies gleamed in the bright light.

In the hallway he passed a few people who gave him peculiar looks. He'd never had much of a poker face. He supposed what he'd discovered was probably evident on his face.

The lunchroom was a place of shadows created by light from the vending machines. The overheads were off. The impression was of stepping into a closet. Doc liked the feeling. It smacked of a kind of protection.

Dinner tonight was no. 3 on the vending menu—instead of salami and cheese or baloney and cheese, he elected ham and cheese. He got a Diet Rite Cola and carried his bounty over to the corner, where a wobbly table awaited him.

For a time he didn't eat. Just blanked his mind and sat there. Listening to the hum and thrum of the vending machines. He could easily imagine them becoming formidable opponents. Big and blocky and deadly. He'd grown up on a farm, when the most amazing thing in sight was a radio that played "Jack

Benny" and "Tom Mix." In those days you sure as hell didn't get your lunch from a machine.

He ate slowly.

The white bread stuck to his mouth like glue and the ham didn't taste like meat at all. But this was arthritis season—his wife's hands gnarled as a monkey's—and he didn't want to impose his needs on her.

Halfway through the sandwich, the door to the lunchroom opened up. A fleshy janitor Doc's own age shuffled in. They'd gone to school together, back in the days when a "bus" took the form of a spavined work horse.

"Hey, hiya Doc," Johnny Dolan said.

Were men their age still called Johnny?

"Hiya, Johnny."

"Another sumptuous meal, huh?"

"Yeah."

"I thought you rich doctors had it made."

"This is one rich doctor who doesn't."

No sense in arguing with people about "rich" doctors. They couldn't afford to pay more than half their Sears bill every month, and credit at the co-op was getting a tad strained . . . but people still perceived him as "rich." And that was all that mattered.

"Hey," Johnny said.

"What?"

"You."

"What about me?"

Johnny came in for a closer look. His gray work clothes were wrinkled. He pushed a mobile bucket ahead of him. It sloshed as it moved.

"You all right?" he said.

"Huh?"

"You don't look so good."

"Oh, yeah," Doc Adams said. So it was obvious. "I'm okay. Just tired."

"You sure?"

"I'm sure."

He was a nice guy, Johnny was, always had been since the days they'd chased hardball flies and dodged cowpies at the same time.

Johnny nodded to the vending machines. "Maybe you should eat something a little better for you." Then he laughed. "Listen to me—givin' advice to a doctor."

"I'll be fine, Johnny. Thanks for thinking about me, though."

In the lonely room his voice was ragged and weary.

Johnny studied him a while longer. Then he got himself a Snickers and a bag of Frito-Lay potato chips. And then he left.

He looked everything over once again, the lab door closed tight behind him, wanting to be sure, absolutely sure.

He had taken tissue samples from Brad Stovik, the truck driver who'd been killed out at the swamp, and then he'd taken samples from the Rydell man who'd been killed by a falling tree limb in front of Windhaven Orphanage four days ago.

He spent the next twenty minutes checking and rechecking his calculations, and suspicions, then he shut down the microscope again and sat back in his chair.

There could be no doubt.

None at all.

He reached for the phone to call the sheriff's department and then he remembered. Diane Baines wasn't sheriff anymore. She'd been fired by his old nemesis, the Stockbridge coalition.

He knew better than to call anybody involved with that bunch. God only knew what they'd do with such information.

He left the lab, closing and locking the door, and walked over to the cubicle that was his office. In his desk drawer he found a phone directory and looked up the Baines woman's phone number.

By now he was thinking about the boy Diane had described to him. There was something strange about him. Diane had at first described the boy as possessing some kind of supernatural—or at least super natural powers—but the longer she'd talked, the less sure she'd become. Finally, both she and Tyler had said that they felt they couldn't be sure of what they'd seen, that everything had happened so quickly. . . .

Diane answered on the third ring. "Yes?"

"This is Doc Adams."

"Hello, Doc."

"Sorry to hear that Stockbridge got rid of you."

She laughed hollowly. "Well, I suppose my life will go on."

"If you need anything—and you know damn well this is a serious offer—you just let me know."

"I appreciate that."

He paused. He was a proud and plain man, one not

211

given to any kind of hysteria, and he was afraid he was going to sound like some talk-show alarmist. But he had to say it. Wasn't the proof in the microscope? "Maybe that Brian boy did have some kind of strange powers, after all, Diane."

He could tell that she, too, was trying to keep her composure. "Why do you sat that?"

He explained.

When he finished, she said, "Are you sure?"

"I'm not sure what it means, I'm not sure what caused it, but I am sure that the tissue has mutated."

"God."

"I know."

"Maybe we should get together. I've got an appointment tonight, but how about tomorrow morning?"

"Fine. It doesn't matter much anyway, now that he's dead, I mean."

"Nine?"

"Great. Why don't you come out to the house?"

"Fine. See you then."

After hanging up, he went back into the lab. He had to look at the tissue sample once again.

Had to.

It was like looking at a miracle.

A terrifying one.

4

A wind creaked the bare trees surrounding the swamp. Below, on the road, cars and trucks hurried through the darkness. It was a good night to be home.

Up here the wind teased at the icy waters. It blew snowdrifts over the jagged rocks surrounding the water's edge and carried litter high in the air, tumbling into the gloom.

Below the surface of the ice, the glow began so faintly that not even eyes close by could have seen it.

Nothing more than a pinprick of light.

Over a ten-minute period it became larger, till it was as round as a dinner plate, and pulsating in its center.

Then the noise began.

At first it sounded like the muffled cry of a youngster.

Then other tones—other cries—joined in, until they blended and became the plaintive wailing sounds of unhappy children.

The sound carried on the winds, wrapping around Windhaven Orphanage below, then carrying on into the town.

A few people out on the icy sidewalks paused to listen more closely, but then they decided it was just a curious sound made by the wind, and they quickly went on with their lives.

Into a drugstore the noise went, and the pharmacist who was locking up glanced around his store in apprehension; then into a tavern where the sound got the attention of several men watching a prize fight, men who could only look at each other curiously, afraid to admit what was going on in their minds; and finally the noise settled in a Catholic Church, where candles flickered in the massive darkness across the body of Christ who looked down so sadly on the lot of humankind. In the shadows Christ seemed to recognize the sounds for what they were, and His eyes seemed all the sadder.

Back at the swamp, the blue glow now suffused the entire area of water.

Ice cracked, melting.

Beneath the surface, the waters churned, roiled. As if in anticipation of something.

A small hand appeared from the water.

The hand reached, as if drowning, for the edge of the water.

Once, twice, three times it reached—all to no avail. Then finally it found purchase on the crusty embankment.

Then the second hand appeared.

Through the blowing snow that stuck to the rough surface of the embankment, the hands proceeded to dig and claw their way upward until hands became arms and arms became shoulders.

Until the head of Brain Courtney appeared.

In all it took five minutes for him to pull himself completely from the water. He came up through the roiling water like something new and terrible being born, escaping its afterbirth.

Then he stood on top of the embankment, his clothes sodden with water, his hair plastered to his face.

His eyes pulsated with the same fierce blue glow as the swamp itself as he turned to look down the hill at the sight of Windhaven Orphanage.

The cries from the swamp filled the air as he stood there in the lashing snow—looking and waiting.

The night was only beginning.

Chapter Ten

1

Diane and Tyler stood in the dark doorway of the bedroom, watching Caroline sleep.

The girl smelled sweetly of childhood slumber. Occasionally she thrashed about, indicating some kind of nightmare, or at least troubled dream, but then she became peaceful again.

Finally, reluctantly, Diane pulled herself away from the doorway.

She felt something she would rather not have—a sense of family shared between herself and Tyler and the sleeping Caroline.

"I'd better get ready," she whispered.

She went on ahead of him into the bathroom where she washed her face, her hands, put on some perfume, and then tugged a clean turtleneck over her head.

In the mirror she noticed the laugh lines around her eyes and mouth.

Old lady, she thought: That's what you're getting to be. She remembered Caroline sleeping, and the good and real sense of family she felt with Tyler and—

But there was too much to do tonight to worry about that.

Anyway, she was going to be a Kate Hepburn old maid, crusty and just overflowing with dignity. . . .

When she got to the kitchen, Tyler was spooning Folgers into the Mr. Coffee. He looked embarrassed when their eyes met. "I should have asked you if it was all right."

She smiled. "You're right, Tyler. I'm really mad."

He shrugged, smiled. "Figured I'd need some of this stuff if I'm going to stay up and baby sit."

They had already decided that she would go meet Coffey at the Dekker farm, and let him watch over Caroline.

"How're you doing?" Diane asked.

He shrugged. "Fair. If I told you I wasn't thinking about taking a drink, I'd be lying."

"Nobody's stopping you."

"I'm stopping me."

She leaned over and kissed him on the cheek. "Actually, I've been cheating."

"Huh?"

"I mean, I haven't come right out and said please don't drink, Tyler, but every few minutes I say a prayer so you won't take one."

"So far it seems to be working."

"So far."

Tyler finished preparing the coffee, then went over to the counter and took a Cheese-It from the box.

218

"I've been thinking about Doc Adams' call."

"So have I."

"What do you think he found out?"

"I don't know. He was very mysterious."

"There was something strange about that kid. That Brian."

"Maybe. Maybe we also hallucinated."

"The tree limb broke."

"That much we know for sure."

"And he brought it down."

"That's the part that's still open to question."

"We saw it."

"We think we saw it," Diane said.

He laughed. "You would have made a great philosophy teacher. We had a chaplain in the Army like you. He was always playing reality games like that. One night he got all of us wondering if we even existed."

She smiled. "Maybe we don't."

He looked at her levelly. "Boy, I sure hope you do."

She flushed. "Thanks."

Then she pecked him on the cheek again and started out the back door to the garage.

She paused a moment. Looked back at Tyler. "You're going to make it, John. You really are."

He smiled. Not without sadness. "You may be right, at that."

He sat in a straight-backed chair that his massive size easily overflowed.

He wore his black suit and his white shirt and his black string tie, his standard accouterments.

But he also wore one other thing—a look of total and utter dejection.

Raymond Stockbridge had no idea what time it was.

Sometime earlier in the evening he had come into his huge den to get away from the stern stares he'd experienced at dinner—the stares of his daughter.

She was still punishing him for what had happened with Davie Mason a few days ago. . . .

Putting his hands on his knees, forcing strength from his back into his arms, he pressed himself to his feet.

In the guttering light of the candles arrayed along the fireplace mantel, images of his past life danced before him. What the people of Haversham had mostly forgotten now was that once he'd actually been slender and handsome . . . and not at all the mountainous being he was now. He lifted a faded black-and-white photograph from the mantel . . . the one that showed him, just after the war standing in a business suit next to a brand-new Chevrolet. His wife, also slender, even beautiful in a slightly off-beat way, stood next to him. She wore a plain summer frock. Only when you looked carefully did you see the swell of her belly. . . .

Within four months their one and only child would be born.

The next picture showed him four years later.

This time he stood in front of a much more expensive car, a shiny Packard. His wife was there also. So was someone else—a small girl whose eyes were mesmeric.

The girl stared straight at the camera, and you could not help but be caught up in her look. It was frightening. In this picture Stockbridge had gained seventy or eighty pounds. He was already becoming unrecognizable from his old photographs. In those days, his underlings—he was already boss of Haversham in every respect—were politely referring to him as "stout."

In the next photograph—depicting him in a silk dressing gown his wife had bought for him in Chicago—he was unmistakably fat. Even gross. No more "stout."

Nobody could have used that word to describe him with a straight face.

His pudgy fingers trembled as he raised the next framed photograph to his eyes. His wife and daughter were standing smiling for the camera in front of a huge Lincoln Continental—while in the background, almost as if the photographer wanted to lose him, stood Stockbridge. He was even, appropriately, out of focus.

The most feared man in Haversham—

If only the public really knew—

As if to assuage his ego, he quickly picked up other photographs, a series of shots that showed him with some of the most influential people in the area—state senators, sports celebrities, media people—these were the photographs he clung to when he felt that his life was out of control.

Then his eyes fell on the final photograph on the mantel, the one he often removed only to find that his daughter always returned it to its "proper" place. It showed him standing out in front of a large, castlelike structure. Midsummer it was, 1957 (you could tell by looking at the plate on a nearby Oldsmobile), and upstate—the clue here was in the spruce trees that did not grow downstate, in Haversham's region. At the edge of the picture was a Plymouth with an MD symbol on its license plate. Near it could be seen a somber-looking Doc Adams. His hair was all brown in those days and he wore a suit slightly too small, and his lopsided stance gave him the air of an absent-minded professor in repose.

Only if you looked carefully could you see the bars on the windows in the building behind Doc Adams.

The bars that had kept Raymond Stockbridge a prisoner for more than six months.

The name of the place had been Pleasant Pines. What an odd name for a mental hospital. . . .

Stockbridge shuddered and set the picture down. He closed his eyes, as if in prayer, and made fists of his huge hands.

For more than six months—

The electro-shock treatment—

The constant questioning—

His eyes came open. There was a wild aspect to them.

And soon the tears came, silver in the light from the fireplace. A huge, blubbery man . . . crying. He knew how pathetic he must look at the moment. Bad enough that he was so fat—even worse that he was fat and so weak. Especially when the whole town imagined him as powerful. . . .

Six months.

It had all begun with the Timmins boy and the tin soldier Stockbridge had given the lad. . . .

A harmless gesture . . .

He wheeled around to see who had come through the door without knocking.

Not that it could be anyone else.

"My God," she said, "get hold of yourself."

He must look especially bad tonight. Even across the room she could see his tears.

She came in closer, masculine in black, eyes flashing behind her rimless glasses, a sneer that was part amusement, part scorn on her lips.

"You're afraid again, aren't you?"

She made it not a gentle question but rather an accusation.

The tears came uncontrollably now as the horrendous man rocked back and forth on his heels.

"Yes," he said, "Afraid."

"Afraid they're going to find out what you did, isn't that right?"

"Yes," he said. "Yes."

He was blubbering now.

Her riding crop appeared as if by magic. She

223

slammed it against the table.

"You need your medicine," she said.

"No, no," he said.

He had already begun to plead.

He hated his medicine. It made his mouth dry and filled his sleep with nightmares.

"No," he said.

But from her jacket pocket she took a bottle. And there was no question what it was.

She threw half a dozen pills across the table. They rattled as they settled on the wood.

"Take them," she said.

"No, please," he said.

She slammed the table once again.

"Take them."

"No—please—I—"

"Do you want me to tell them what you did?"

"My God," he said. "Please, listen—"

"You wouldn't like that would you?"

"No, I—listen—please—"

"Then take them. Take them now. Take all of them."

He paused, looking down at the pills strewn across the table. He raised his eyes and hands in a kind of informal prayer.

And then he picked up one of the pills, opened his mouth, and swallowed it.

He did not need to look at his daughter to see what she was doing.

Her smile of satisfaction would only make the moment more terrible.

The car heater made a noise only slightly less furious than a B-52 as it rolled along the asphalt road toward the Dekker farm.

A sheen of ice covered the moonlit road. Diane had to use both hands on the wheel and resist the temptation to hit the brakes as the car slid around some sleek curves.

A lonely saxophone solo filled her ears. Images of Tyler and Caroline filled her mind.

If only life were so simple—inheriting an instant family and living happily ever after.

But there were too many unresolved matters, not the least of which were the disturbing deaths of Davie Mason and Brian Courtney—and the strange events of that morning when Brian seemed to tear a tree apart with nothing more than a beam from his finger.

But no. That was impossible.

Moonlight through the window fell on the Smith and Wesson on the seat. She had returned her badge, her various forms of identification, even her mileage notebook, which the county supervisors had requested she keep.

But the weapon was hers.

She'd had a special handle fitted for her and paid for it herself.

It was hers and she wasn't about to let it go.

The Dekker farm had been closed during the worst of the agricultural recession a few years back.

Now it lay like the last remnant of a ghost town, a silhouette against the soft night sky, full moon in back, clouds dragging past. The outbuildings were dark hulks as she pulled onto the slick gravel surface of driveway. Fencing dragged to the ground. The headlights swept past a barn in need of paint and a house that birds, animals, and kids with rocks had managed to turn into a fallen temple.

In a horseshoe drive on the east side of the house a man sat inside a big Chevy van.

Coffey.

She shut off her engine and got out.

She liked the sense of isolation out here. The trains roaring in the distance; the dogs yipping. The way the cold nipped at her nose and cheeks. It reminded her of girlhood, romantic walks, snowball fights, snowmen with noses of coal.

The effect was somewhat spoiled when Coffey got out of his truck carrying a shotgun.

"Howdy."

"Howdy," she said.

Coffey always said that. It wasn't an affectation. Coming from him, bulky, blocky, a comfortable, jocky kind of man, it seemed perfectly natural.

"I don't usually answer mystery phone calls," she said.

"Figured you'd come about this one. Given all that's happened."

She was curious about his exact implication. "All what?"

"The cover-up."

"I'm not following you, Mr. Coffey."

He stood in the silver light of the evening, his face lost in shadows, his body hidden beneath a sheep-lined jacket.

"The cover-up. The deaths of the boys."

"You're saying they were—" She paused.

"I'm saying they were murders, and I'm saying you were fired because you were going to investigate them and discover the truth."

"You know the truth?"

"I know a part of it."

She shook her head. "You're making me feel like I'm drunk, Mr. Coffey. I'm not following you at all."

He nodded to the barn.

"Fifteen years ago, after that kid was killed in a hit-and-run accident, a couple of us on the council hired a private eye to find out what the Stockbridge clan wouldn't—who really ran over that boy."

"And what did you find?"

"That's what I'm about to show you."

He nodded to the barn again.

"Let's go," he said. Then he shook his head. "But before I get too high and mighty about the other people on the council, I better remind myself that I should have done this fifteen years ago."

They walked through the night that smelled of cold and pine trees and old hay in the barn.

He went up to the door and put a shoulder to it and slid it open.

From inside floated the tangy odor of ancient horse

dung. The Dekkers had loved horses.

She followed him past the stalls, into the deepest and darkest part of the barn.

From inside his sheepskin jacket he produced a flashlight the size of a small ballbat. He shone it on the floor as he walked several paces ahead of her. He moved carefully, flashing the light, keeping his eyes scanning the floor.

Obviously he was looking for something. But what was there to find on a barn floor that had been deserted for several years?

"Here," he said.

He fell to his knees with an air of excitement, as if he'd just discovered a trunk of pirate gold.

"Hold this," he said grumpily.

He held the light out to her. She took it, playing it across the area where his hands worked.

In five minutes he had it open, a crevice in the earth that was hidden by a door attached flat to the ground.

"Ready?" he said.

"For what?"

"For what?" he asked, sounding startled. "Why for going down the ladder."

She shuddered. "I'll be damned," she said. "I'll be damned."

4

Caroline.

In her dream the voice was stronger and stronger.

Caroline.

She ran.

Stumbled.

Fell.

Caroline.

She was not sure what pursued her, only that she was running down a narrow tunnel at the end of which pulsed a yellowish, foggy light.

The voice did not seem to have a shape of any kind. It simply floated, like the fog, pressing at her, threatening her in some way she could not understand.

Caroline.

Then she awoke.

Her head snapped upward so quickly that she pulled several of the long muscles in her neck and touched her hand to the source of the pain.

Gradually, lying down flat again, her eyes got used to the deep shadows of the room.

Diane's room.

The only place Caroline had felt at home in many long years.

She wished Diane were here, hugging her, holding her, the way she had that afternoon. For that wonderful moment it had been easy to imagine that Diane was her mother . . . and that she had at last found a home.

The wind came up; thoughts of Diane faded.

She felt alone again, abandoned, even though in the dim light she could see the stuffed animals and smell the wonderful perfume.

Images of the dream returned—the tunnel, the desperate attempt to get away from the voice, the curious light that she ran and ran toward without ever quite reaching.

The wind again; she relaxed, feeling snug under the top blanket. She was in socks and underwear and a blouse.

Getting sleepy again . . .

She tried not to drift off. . . .

When she awoke she was sweating again, entangled in a nightmare again, so for nearly a full minute she couldn't be sure that what she saw in her window was real. . . .

A creature with glowing eyes—

A blue glow—

She slapped her hands over her eyes, afraid that this was no nightmare at all—

When she looked again the window was empty, except for a naked tree on a hillside blowing in the bitter wind.

She sat up, sticky with sweat.

Caroline—

A single white hand appeared on the other side of the glass, as if it were clawing to get in.

Caroline—

The hand disappeared, and in its place the eerie pale oval of a face pressed to the pane.

Caroline stifled a shriek. It was Brian. His hair was plastered to his skull, his skin vaguely iridescent, his eyes haunted and glowing with a faint blue tone like that of the chemical dump's surface, but it was Brian. Alive.

Caroline—

She needed no command to know why he was here, what he wanted.

No words were necessary between them to tell her what they would do tonight.

There was work to do.

Oh, yes, there was work to do.

All Diane could think of was the catacombs of ancient Rome where the early Christians had been forced to hide.

Coffey's voice echoed up to her as he preceded her down the ladder that seemed to drop endlessly into a black well that waited to engulf her.

She gripped the rungs of the ladder tightly, afraid she might get vertigo. It was a long way to fall and very narrow—playing directly on two of her worst fears.

"Steady now," Coffey said in an old-coot voice.

"I'm all right," Diane said.

Was that a snort she heard in response?

Whatever, she didn't have time to worry about it at this point.

The more rungs she descended, the more the walls were stained with moisture, the more the air became dark with dampness.

The only light was the beam from the flashlight. From the sound below her, she could tell that Coffey had reached the bottom and was holding the light upward for her.

The damp smell got worse. It was like having your face wrapped in a wool blanket that had been left to mildew.

Finally, she reached the last rung. For a moment

her foot dangled, then she jumped down.

Coffey was there with a supporting hand.

He shone the light around the room in which they stood, and she stared amazed, at what lay before her.

A little girl's room that had once been as precious and sentimental as something almost sickeningly sweet on a greeting card.

There was a canopied bed, a huge doll house, a rocking horse, a large portable closet filled with expensive dresses. If you overlooked where the room was housed, you would have to say that a very lucky little girl had lived here.

"What is this place?" Diane asked.

"I'm not sure. Not exactly."

Diane looked around again. She was just as baffled the second time over. "Did somebody actually live here?"

Coffey didn't say anything.

Instead he crossed the bedroom floor and pushed the portable closet out of the way.

There lay a door built into the rock wall.

He turned back to her and said, "Did anybody ever tell you how Mrs. Kilrane's brother died?"

She smiled thinly. "You're making me feel drunk again. I'm not sure what you're talking about."

He came over and sat on the edge of the bed. Dust rose from the frilly pink and white spread. Springs creaked.

"Lavonne Stockbridge's twin brother was named Robert. One day when he was nine years old, he stood in the third floor of Windhaven Orphanage and apparently fell to his death. Accidental death, everyone assumed at the time."

He paused, blowing into his hands. In addition to being damp down here, it was also cold.

Diane stood away from the bed. With the raised floor, the specially built walls that did not quite cover the whole wall nor quite reach the ceiling, the place made her think of a movie set.

Coffey shivered inside his big sheep-lined jacket.

"Anyway, over the years there was speculation about what really might have happened—apparently, Raymond Stockbridge must have wondered, too, because I think he kept Mrs. Kilrane down here for a long, long time when she was a girl."

All Diane could think of was the tin soldier. The one that Caroline had gotten from Brian Courtney. The one that John Tyler had found on the small boy who'd been the hit-and-run victim.

"Does any of it make sense to you?"

"Not much of it," Coffey admitted. He nodded to the door. "I do know where that leads."

"Where?"

"Windhaven."

"The orphanage?"

He frowned, nodded.

"God," she said.

Her mind was alive with speculation, all of it frightening, most of it depressing.

Diane moved into the bedroom. She ran a gloved hand along the edge of the canopied bed. She stared idly at herself in the full-length mirror. She touched one of the sweet, frilly little dresses hanging inside the portable closet. She touched the wooden horse, rocking it gently. The she opened one of the bureau drawers and peeked inside.

"May I borrow your flashlight?"

"Sure," he said, handing it to her.

When she shone the light down into the empty drawer, she was reminded again of the fact that they were really in a cave.

Shadows loomed, consumed her.

She played the beam on yellowed newsprint lining the bottom of the drawer, then lifted up a piece of it, and checked the date.

March 14, 1952.

The stuff was more than thirty years old!

Quickly, she went through the other drawers, finding similar vintages on the newspaper linings.

She wasn't sure what her finding meant, just that in some way it was significant.

Finished, she put several pieces of newsprint in her pocket. Then she turned back to Coffey.

"You seem real excited about something," he said.

"I am."

"What?"

"I don't know."

"Boy, that's a good one."

She laughed. "I'm sorry, but I'm going to have to think some things through." She handed him back his flashlight. "How did you find out this place was down here?"

"When they auctioned off the Dekker place," he said. "I almost bought it. I've always thought of retiring to a farm. Just say the hell with all the pressures and get to know the earth a little better."

"Sounds nice."

"So anyway, when this place went up for sale, I came out here, really looked it over careful. I was checking out the barn when I stumbled onto the trap door. Then I came down here and—"

"You said you should have reported this a long time ago."

"Yeah."

"Why?"

"Because something tells me it's got something to do with the deaths of kids who've been at Windhaven. You know, once in a while a few of them would disappear and never be found—this was in addition to the ones who got involved in 'accidents.' I should've reported this right away, but I was scared."

"Of Stockbridge?"

"Of what his power could do to me. I'm close to retirement age. I've got a wife who isn't in the best of health. I need my money. If Stockbridge ever decided to wipe me out, it wouldn't be any trouble at all for him, believe me."

"I know," she said solemnly.

"But given that the door leads to Windhaven and all, and given the disappearances over the years, I think I should bring this up with the proper authorities." He shrugged. "Until today, I guess that was you."

"I guess it was."

They looked around the room once more, the flashlight playing over the oddly touching display of little-girl things.

Which was when it happened.

The door above them slammed closed, the sound of it echoing off the walls.

For a moment, neither of them said anything, only

listened in shock to the reverberations of the falling door.

Then he said, "Somebody's gonna have some fun—at our expense."

He shone his light up along the rungs of the ladder, up to where the door had slammed.

"Gonna be a long night," he said.

He had just finished speaking when the door opened up.

Diane only had time to catch a glimpse of somebody in a ski-mask before the shooting started.

Both of them had to dive for cover before another round was fired.

"Evening, Sheriff."

Deputy Farnsworth still couldn't get used to it. Being called sheriff.

He had just walked inside the 7-11 (the Christmas decorations were already up, cardboard Santas peering from displays of beer and candies) when the cashier, a pimply kid who liked to spend his time collecting brownie points, greeted him with the "sheriff" acknowledgment.

"Evening," Farnsworth said back.

The cashier watched carefully as Farnsworth collected several things in a hand carrier—bread, soup, milk . . . and Sominex.

Farnsworth came up and set them down on the counter.

The cashier gave him a big smile and went to work as if he were taking a PhD in cash registering.

Farnsworth stared dully behind the kid at the new issue of *Penthouse*.

Instead of inspiring lust, the magazine only reminded him of how far away Diane Baines was now—and forever.

An indiscretion several years earlier—what some might have called a little too much enthusiasm for some of the county funds kept in the sheriff's office—was the leverage the Stockbridge family had on him.

And it was leverage enough to see that he would do four-to-seven downstate and ruin his life.

"Hell, just take a little beer."

Farnsworth's eyes came back into focus and settled on the kid. "What—sorry."

"Said you don't need these. Hell, I just watch a couple minutes of Hawaii Five-O, sip a little beer, and I knock off to sleep in no time."

The kid, who apparently was old enough to drink beer, suddenly came clear to Farnsworth. This kid sounded like the son of Barney Fife on the old "Andy Griffith Show." A know-it-all.

"Oh, yeah, well maybe I'll try that."

"This stuff doesn't work, anyway."

"Well, let's just ring it up for the hell of it, all right?"

The edge of menace in the sheriff's otherwise soft voice was obvious.

"Yeah, sure," the kid said.

He finished ringing up the sheriff's order without saying another word.

When the sheriff said good night, all Barney's son said was, "Yup."

Farnsworth sat in his car outside the 7-11 staring in.

He was so tired he could scarcely move—the past two days had been a jumble of wearing circumstances, not the least of which was the irretrievable loss of Diane Baines as at least his friend and certainly as his would-be lover—but now he couldn't sleep.

For the past four hours he'd lain in bed and tried to do it, but he couldn't. Insomnia was a special form of hell.

He had been forced to relive his life, and it had not been a happy experience. All he ended up with were the facts that he was thirty-eight, unmarried, lonely . . . and caught in a kind of spiritual drift he could neither understand nor control.

He happened to glance up and see the kid in the 7-11 staring curiously at him.

It was a good bet that, by dawn, that kid would have told at least two dozen people about how "weird" the sheriff had been acting tonight.

Then he, and his listeners, would begin speculating on just why, and in what way, the sheriff was so "weird."

Irritated, Farnsworth pulled the car into gear and pulled out of the parking lot.

The kid kept right on staring.

7

There was the night and the wind and the strange boy whom she followed through a section of woods that became increasingly dark and impenetrable.

He was Brian Courtney—and he was also somebody else.

Already, she had skinned her knee from falling, and her lungs seared from the pace Brian kept up, but Caroline ran after him anyway.

Sometimes there were puddles she splashed through; sometimes there were deep embankments of snow she had to wade through. But she kept going, in a trance, true, but this was no dream as her frozen skin and runny nose and pounding heart attested.

All she could do, all she wanted to do, was follow.

She had no idea how long they'd been running when Brian crested a hill and stopped.

By the time she reached him, she was forced to drop to her knees, her jeans soaked, her face raw from exposure.

Behind Brian glowed the safety lights of a railroad yard. Distantly she heard boxcars coupling and uncoupling. The noise sounded huge and threatening in the night.

For a long time, neither of them said anything,

only let the night sounds of stray animals and the men below in the railroad yard float past their ears.

She took this opportunity to study Brian's face.

From outside her bedroom, a blue tint had burned just below the surface of his skin. That remained, now, along with his dully staring eyes. She'd seen somebody hypnotized on TV once. That was what Brian looked like now. No expression. Just staring.

"We all thought you'd drowned, Brian," she said, struggling to her knees.

Nothing, he said nothing.

She found her feet, moved closer to him.

"Are you all right?" she asked.

In the silence she could hear the sounds from the railroad yards again. The cold night seemed vast, the sky an inverted black ocean, limitless as God. She felt much older than she ever had, and tired in a way that was more mental than physical.

This time when she spoke to Brian, she put out her hand. "You should have Doc Adams check you over, Brian."

She took his hand.

He didn't jerk away.

He didn't curse her.

He just stood there.

Unmoving.

Uncaring.

She let her hand drop from his and touched his clothes. She shuddered. They were wet. Then, in the red railroad light behind him, she saw that his hair was wet, too.

She shuddered, a startling image jarring her.

Had Brian just come from the swamp?

Had Brian been under the ice all this time?

She huddled into herself. A train hooted behind the first westerly rise. An owl joined in. Indeed, this night felt vast to her. And scarey.

"I want to help you, Brian."

Still nothing.

A note of panic in her voice—he hadn't moved, not an inch, not a muscle—she said, "I'm going to go get Doc Adams, Brian. You really need somebody to help you."

She assumed this would get some kind of response from him and she was right.

Only not the one she'd hoped for.

His hand shot out and seized hers.

She screamed. Pain shot up her arm and seemed to go all the way into her neck and then into her head.

She had never known anybody—of any age—who was as strong as Brian seemed at this minute.

"Please, Brian, you're hurting me."

But he didn't let go.

His dead eyes were turned on hers, holding her through his gaze as he held her physically with his hand.

She started to cry.

She couldn't help it—was even a little embarrassed about it (she prided herself on being just as tough as most boys, in fact much tougher than some of those who bragged about how tough they were in an effort to cover up their cowardice)—but now she couldn't help herself.

The pain was too much.

"Please, Brian," she moaned.

Then he stopped. Just like that.

She spent the next few minutes rubbing her hand, arm, and shoulder.

While she did this, Brian turned away.

He walked over a few feet to the edge of the hill. From here you looked down on the whole of Haversham. Against a backdrop of snow, the small town looked pastoral, several church steeples rising into the sky, a business district built around a town square with a bandstand, blocks and blocks of houses with lazy, comfortable smoke wafting up from chimneys into the night sky.

As Caroline continued to rub her arm for circulation, she saw that Brian's body began to tremble.

At first it was scarcely noticeable, but then the shakes became spasms and spasms tremors.

She forgot about her arm and ran up to him.

Just before she reached him, he began making a growling noise.

She stopped, suddenly afraid to get any nearer.

"Brian?"

For a moment, he clamped his hands to his head and she could see that the headache was back. He writhed in agony, twisting, turning, kicking out.

Finally, the pain seemed to recede. He sat still, staring out at the night. Then, without words:

Help me.

Help you how, Brian?

They're evil, Caroline.

Who?

The people in the town.

Not all of them.

They want me to kill them.

Who wants you to?

The children in the swamp.

Brian, listen, Doc Adams could—

Doc Adams can't help me. You're the only one who can help me. You.

Then she saw him slam his hands to his temples. The headache was returning.

Caroline was terrified.

He shook even more deeply than he had before.

Help me, Caroline. The children want revenge.

As if to prove his point, he rose up and let his vision fall on the boxcar of a nearby train.

Moments later, the boxcar ignited like so much kindling.

Caroline started crying. Brian put his hand out. After a long hesitation, she took it. It was ice cold.

Chapter Eleven

1

Dodge did not wear his usual white attire. Instead he was dressed for working in secret at night—black ski-mask, black turtleneck, black slacks.

His cheeks were ruddy from the outdoors. His dark eyes showed not a trace of their typical amusement.

He looked, uncharacteristically, nervous.

"You're sure they didn't get a look at you?"

"I'm positive," he said.

Mrs. Kilrane came away from the long windows that overlooked the northernmost side of the swampy area that bordered Windhaven Orphanage.

The way she was dressed, few in Haversham would have recognized her. Blue silk lounging pajamas that looked as if they'd been lifted from a 1937 Myrna Loy movie flattered Mrs. Kilrane's angular body in a surprisingly sensuous way. Lipstick, rouge, and eyeliner took away her sexlessness and left her, if not beautiful, at the very least, pleasant looking.

Her desk had been cleared of its calendar, pen and pencil set, and Rolodex. In their place was an expensive silver serving tray, two glasses, and a carafe of good wine.

She filled two goblets carefully and gracefully handed one to Dodge.

She felt something she rarely felt for this man— affection. His experience of half an hour ago had left him shaken—and that gave him a vulnerability she'd never seen before in him. It forced her to admit to herself that she cared more about this man than she'd realized.

Ken Dodge had come to the orphanage fifteen years before . . . right after the disappearance of her husband. At first she'd dismissed him as nothing more than a fading jock, which he was, having played semi-pro football until the team folded. He had an education degree, so he could teach the students in several subjects, and he was good at sports, so he was also useful for encouraging competitive games.

But as for anything else . . .

He'd started out by flattering her . . . and she was more intrigued than wooed by his advances. She took such care to seem sexless, even repellent . . . why would he try to seduce her?

She had dismissed him as either sadistic, wanting to hurt her feelings, or as some kind of pervert—and she wanted nothing to do with him.

But gradually, gradually she found herself doing little things to make herself look better for their occasional late-night staff meetings. Then one night it had happened. It had been so long she was overpowered by the moment. She'd invited him into her office after the others had gone and . . . and within five minutes she found herself on the floor, her dress round her hips, Ken Dodge deep within her, treating her with a wonderful mixture of violence and tenderness. She had never known sex like that before—a howling, frenzied state of being that was as much madness as anything.

The amazing thing was that, four years later, he could still help duplicate that original moment for her.

She sensed that tonight, however, he would not be able to give her what she needed.

He was too upset.

"Maybe I should have shot them," he said, "instead of just firing warning shots."

"You did the right thing. There would have been too many questions."

He looked at her solemnly. "There are going to be questions, anyway."

She sipped her wine. Walked back to the window. Gazed out on the night. Windswept snow gave the swampy area the look of a tundra.

She knew what Dodge was worried about, of course. His investment. While she was convinced that the man did, in his somewhat remote way, care about her, she had no doubt why he stayed here at Windhaven. Eventually her father would die and she would inherit all his holdings. Ken Dodge planned to help her run Haversham. She had no objections to this. He would be good at carrying out her orders— she was not lying to herself when she said she was the cleverer of the two, merely stating an objective fact—and he would be good for her emotionally, too. But now he saw that his investment was in some jeopardy.

"We need to do something," he said.

"I know." She continued to look out the window. Ever since Davie Mason's "accident," the tenuous grasp her family had on Haversham had become even more tenuous. First Sheriff Diane Baines started asking suspicious questions—then she enlisted ex-Sheriff Tyler to help her—then Coffey started asking the council to look into certain things, and . . .

All she could think of was the tin soldier her father had given Davie Mason . . .the same way he'd given the tin soldier to other boys at Windhaven in the past. . . .

She shuddered.

If the town of Haversham ever knew the secrets surrounding her father . . . the stay in the mental hopsital being just one example—if they ever found out, it was doubtful that any Stockbridge would stay in control of Haversham very long.

She was about to speak again when her phone buzzed. She looked at it with an expression of dread. This late at night it would have to be bad news.

"Mrs. Kilrane?"

"Yes."

"No news on Caroline Hayes."

She could not control her temper. "I told you to call me when there was news. You don't need to check in every half-hour with these idiotic reports!"

"Yes, Mrs. Kilrane."

She slammed the phone down.

Now she was as tense as Ken Dodge. She thought again of the past few days . . . Ken having to set fire to Gus Fenster's trailer . . . Brian Courtney and the freak phenomenon (whatever it was) that had killed that little fag Mr. Rydell . . . and Coffey the council-man beginning to vent his longstanding resentment of her and her family.

She felt something she rarely did—self-pity. As if she were at the mercy of forces she could neither understand nor control.

Then suddenly she realized the significance of the phone call a few moments ago.

How it all played into the events of the past few days.

"Caroline Hayes," she said.

"What about her?"

She came back from the window and sat in the tall chair behind her desk. She poured herself more wine.

"She was a good friend of Brian Courtney's, wasn't she?"

"Yes."

"He probably would have confided in her."

"Probably."

"He might have told her about the toy soldier."

"God, I didn't think—"

She slammed her glass so hard that wine spilled all over her hand.

She shook her head miserably. Some of the effects of the makeup were lost now. Worry had given her an ugly look.

"God only knows what my father told Brian. My father gets crazy, he—" She stopped herself, not wanting to think of the implications of her words.

"The only person who can harm us is Caroline Hayes. She might testify against us."

Ken Dodge put down his wine. "We'd better find her."

"Damn," she said. "I can't believe all this is happening."

He looked old and sad and defeated in the dim light of the office. "I can," he said. "My whole life's been this way."

He stood up. He seemed angry now, and feeding on that anger. "Tomorrow morning we start."

"Start what?"

"Looking for Caroline Hayes."

Diane found Tyler sprawled on the kitchen floor.

The first thing she noticed about him was that his gray-flecked hair showed traces of having been burned.

His breathing was shallow and his body sticky with sweat.

Coffey helped her lift the man and move him onto her bed.

Which was when Diane noticed that Caroline was gone and so were her clothes.

Half an hour later, Tyler finished relating the events of the past couple hours.

The eerie blue light he'd seen at Caroline's window.

The sudden bolt of power that had knocked him out.

And the sense that what he was witnessing here was exactly what he'd seen at the orphanage the other day when the teacher Mr. Rydell had been killed.

"Brian," Diane said.

"I didn't see him," Tyler said, "but I don't know who else it could have been."

"But isn't that boy the boy who's dead?" Coffey wanted to know.

Diane and Tyler glanced at each other.

"Yes," Diane said.

Half an hour later the three of them sat at the kitchen table, sharing coffee and a package of sweet rolls Diane had basted with butter and stuck briefly in the microwave.

Coffey pawed at his eyes. "You get my age, a night like this could kill you."

"You're hanging in there just fine," Diane smiled. "And anyway, I think you exaggerate about your age. I've seen you tear down a motor. It's a pretty impressive sight."

Tyler stared at his fists.

"Are you still with us, John?" Diane asked.

"I'm just trying to figure out where he might have taken her."

"Caroline?"

"Yes."

"I don't think we have to worry about him hurting her. She's his best friend."

"Yes," Tyler said. "But what we saw the other day—" He shook his head.

Coffey helped himself to another roll.

"I'm going to the council meeting this morning," he said between bites. "Anybody joining me?"

"The council meeting?"

"Yes, indeed," Coffey said. His spirits had soared. He sounded happier than Diane had ever heard him. "And I'm going to put it right on the table for them. I'm going to talk about the weird little room in the basement of Dekker's barn—I'm going to talk about

254

the suppressed information in the hit-and-run case fifteen years ago—and I'm going to demand a new investigation into the death of David Mason."

Tyler whistled. "That's going to be something to see."

"It's long past due," Coffey said. "I grew up in this community and I love it and I sure as hell don't like what we've let it become."

Diane reached across and patted his hand. "I take it you wouldn't mind company."

"I sure wouldn't," Coffey grinned. "Especially the company of a pretty lady."

"You've got a date, then."

Their good mood lasted a few more minutes. Then slowly the gravity of what they were talking about sank in.

If Raymond Stockbridge had gotten desperate enough to fire on them last night, what might he do after they confronted the entire council with their accusations of Stockbridge wrongdoing?

3

Singing.

He couldn't believe it.

And the song issuing from between his lips—
"When the moon hits your eye like a big pizza
pie/That's Amore"—he hadn't heard let alone sung
since the last time Dean Martin had joined him on
the radio with it . . . and that had to be mid-1950s.

He didn't even mind shaving with the Lady
Gillette she used on her legs.

In fact there was something downright kinky and
erotic about it, something that made him feel even
closer to Emma.

With the shower running—Emma inside, luxuri-
ously soaping her Rubenesque body—with the song
on his lips, he forgot all about the unpleasant parts of
his life.

His marriage to Irna. How she'd turned their
children against him until he was reduced to a
whining, simpering nobody in his own home. How
he was nothing more than a token mayor, with the
Stockbridge family being the real rulers. And how
he'd participated in a felony (an outright felony) the
other day by helping plant drugs in Sheriff Baines'
house.

Ex-Sheriff Baines now . . . thanks, in part, to him
and what he'd done.

He blanked his mind a moment.

Forgot about having to face his wife in less than an hour . . . forgot about the pending council meeting where once again he'd have to belittle and degrade himself in order to please others.

The shower door opened.

Through the rolling steam he glimpsed her . . . her sumptuous, curvaceous body.

He put down the razor and went into the shower with her.

Neither spoke.

He pressed her gently back against the wall of the shower and let his hand—almost as if it were guided by an unseen force, so urgent was his love—find the tender warmth between her legs.

The water pounded against him, cleansing him, stirring him.

He eased himself up inside her. She seemed to envelop him entirely, possess him in some way he'd never been possessed before.

They found an easy rhythm as his hands covered her buttocks, as one of her large breasts swam into his mouth. This was the love he'd always looked for . . . part fondness, part lust. He was so hard he felt as if a kind of madness had overtaken him. Orgasm was not only a pleasant experience . . . it was necessary to his sanity.

He was thinking all these things when the door opened up and through the steam he saw a figure clad in black wielding a butcher knife, off whose blunt edge sparkled a hellish light.

Emma must have seen it, too, because even before the black-clad figure, whose identity was lost in the rolling steam—even before the figure could move closer, Emma began to scream.

Elliot had no idea what to do.

His mind was filled with a terrible headline—one that would humiliate both his wife, his children and his mother—MAYOR DIES IN SHOWER MURDER.

My God, Elliot thought. My God.

But suddenly he had other concerns.

Because it was then that the long butcher knife began slashing the air only inches from his shoulder.

4

"The cells," Doc Adams said, "have mutated."

Diane frowned. "I guess I don't know what that means."

He smiled unhappily. "Neither do I."

They stood in the vestibule of the rambling ancient house that also doubled as his office. Both had agreed that meeting at the morgue was a bad idea. Too many people would see them, get curious about what was going on.

Doc Adams's place smelled sweet this morning. After Diane had entered, he'd explained that his wife had just finished serving them a breakfast of pancakes with homemade maple syrup. He'd asked if Diane had wanted any, but she'd declined.

Now they sat in a small office filled with filing cabinets and unruly stacks of medical journals.

Doc Adams was hunched over a cluttered desk, resting on one elbow, tapping a pencil on a page filled with notes he'd taken.

"So our suspicions were right, Diane. Something very odd is going on here with that Brian Courtney kid."

Then she told him about Tyler's experience glimpsing Brian at the window last night—and Caroline's disappearing.

Doc Adams surprised her by not seeming surprised

259

at all.

He simply looked at his notes and said, "You have any explanations?"

"No."

He continued to study his notes, then threw his pencil over them, as if he were giving up. "I only know one thing—starting with that truck driver, Stovik, who stopped at the swampy area a few days ago, and ending with Mr. Rydell, there seems to have been some kind of radiation loose in Haversham. That's what the mutation is all about—an accelerated growth of white cells. And by accelerated, I'm talking about an abnormal growth rate that might normally take twenty or thirty years taking place over a few hours. I don't have anything to compare it to."

All she could think of was Brian.

So it hadn't been a hallucination.

Softly, she said, "We're going to the council this morning."

He just looked at her. Sucked on his dead pipe. "I wondered when somebody around here was going to come to their senses."

She explained all the things they were going to confront the council with. "Then it's up to them. Either they let us look into the deaths of the children or we go to the state attorney's office for help. It'll be up to them."

He nodded back to his notes. He looked as if he had something to say but was reluctant. "I'm sure you're familiar with how chemicals preserve things."

She nodded. "Sure. The way we preserve food, you mean?"

"Essentially, yes."

He offered only an embarrassed silence.

"You want to say something, don't you?"

"I may have a theory about what's going on at the chemical dump. A partial theory, anyway."

"Then say it."

He smiled self-consciously. "I'm supposed to be a crusty old doctor, not a wild-eyed radical." He paused. "Well, say, just for the sake of argument, that kids got tossed in that chemical dump and that the dump had just the right mix of chemicals to preserve—"

"You mean they're alive?"

"Maybe not alive as we know it."

"Do you really believe that?"

"Let's just say I'm not ruling it out."

All she could do was stare at him.

Five minutes later he walked her to the front door. "Thanks for all your help, Doc. I'll keep your theory in mind—and I'll let you know how I come out at the council."

He smiled wearily. "They're going to fight you, you know."

"I know."

"And when they're mad, no telling what they'll do."

She nodded.

He took her hand. Squeezed it. "Be careful. And feel free to use my name in any way you think is helpful."

She leaned over. Kissed him on the cheek.

When she stood erect again she saw a small, pretty

gray-haired woman in the doorway. The woman was smiling. "It's a good thing I'm not the jealous sort."

Diane returned her smile. "You should be, Mrs. Adams. You've got quite a catch for yourself here."

As she started through the doorway, the smaller woman touched her arm and said, "Good luck with the council today."

Diane's jaw set. "Unfortunately, I have the feeling we're going to need it."

5

There was only one thing he could do. And he did it.

Elliot Hughes lowered his head and plowed right into the midsection of the black-clad assailant who had walked into Emma's shower.

Emma was still screaming.

The assailant was still slashing the knife through the air.

Elliot lunged hard, and came in low enough under the knife, like a lineman making a textbook-perfect tackle.

The assailant went flying backward, the butcher knife tumbling upward through the air, sharp edges gleaming, and the big floppy black hat that somehow looked familiar went tumbling too.

The hat.

For a moment it mesmerized him, to the exclusion of all else.

The hat: Why did it look so familiar?

About the time he began to understand the implications of the hat, his body—without any urging from his mind—pounced on the assailant, raised its fist and was about to break a jaw or a nose or both when the screaming started in earnest again.

Only this time it wasn't Emma who was screaming—instead, it was the assailant.

"Shit," Elliot said. "Shit."

"What is it?" Emma shouted hysterically, trying to cover up her amplitude with a towel.

"This—person."

"What about him?" Emma asked.

"It isn't a him."

"It's a her?"

"Yes, it's a her."

"God," Emma said, "God."

Which was exactly what Elliot was thinking, because there on the floor, beneath him, was none other than his wife, Irna.

He had never seen her so silent or so sullen.

Never.

After he finished vomiting, Caroline helped Brian up into the boxcar.

Full day had come, a mean, overcast day that inspired mean, overcast moods.

In the trainyard engineers jumped from one train to another, yard clerks checked locked cars, furtive, sad-eyed hobos flitted from one shadow to another.

The boxcar where they sat smelled of urine and feces. Obviously, others had used it before them.

She had taken off her coat and wrapped it around Brian.

He sat staring dully into the darkness that collected at the top of the boxcar.

His eyes were normal, his skin was no longer tainted blue.

He looked like the familiar Brian, except for his pasty skin. He was obviously sick.

"They won't let me alone," he said. "I want to help them, but they scare me."

She took his hand. "We won't let them get you, Brian. I promise."

"They're angry."

"I know."

"They were murdered."

She nodded.

"They want revenge."

"Then we should go to the police."

"I—I'm afraid of what they might do if I tried that."

She looked at him. "Brian, you're free of them now. Whatever power they had over you is gone."

He looked at her skeptically. With his lank hair, his wrinkled clothes, his sickly skin, he was a boy obviously in need of help.

"We'll go see Diane Baines," she said. "She can help us."

"They don't like any adults. Don't trust them."

"But—"

But she knew it would do no good to keep talking. Better let him rest for now.

In moments, he was asleep, his head against her shoulder.

She thought of how he'd described his days below the surface of the chemical waters in the swamp.

Brian understood that at the end of the long corridor of white light there was a gentler and better world.

Yet he could not go to that world—nor could any of the children—until his business on the surface was finished.

For days he existed in a turmoil of images from his other life—he saw Mr. Stockbridge's tin soldier marching, his limbs moving in precise military fashion, marching endlessly, if seemed, until suddenly his eyes and mouth ran with blood and he fell over dead. He saw the woman in the dime store photograph whom he'd pretended was his mother come alive within the picture frame and speak to him: "There is a more peaceful world, Brian, a world of floating consciousness where you will understand everything and know peace and love. I will be your mother, Brian. I will be your mother, Brian. I will be your mother."

And he saw the children—the brutalized and maimed corpses of the children killed at Windhaven—each remarkably preserved. When he was six Brian had gone to a circus and seen Siamese twins floating in a big jar filled with pink water. They had seemed alive, though he knew they had been dead for years. Here, too, the children seemed alive. Seen through eerie light blue water they floated, their hair trailing like seaweed, their dead eyes blank and unseeing, their mouths gaping black holes. Yet they communicated as Brian learned to communicate with thoughts rather than words, their childish souls trapped in bodies never at peace.

There was a better world. All he needed to do was take the proper vengeance to reach it—for himself, and for the children in the swamp.

Caroline sat watching Brian sleep.

There was no doubt at all now what the children wanted Brian to do. No doubt, either, that he was going to be forced to do it. She imagined, just as Brian had described it, the destruction of Windhaven and Haversham. Men, women, children fleeing down firestorm streets the way napalm victims had once fled down rural roads in Viet Nam . . . flames crawling up their backs.

This was what the voices demanded.

And Brian was chosen to carry it out.

A few minutes later, she herself drifted off. The past two days had been the most frantic and confusing of her life, and now she was utterly exhausted.

When she woke, not long from then, she was disoriented. The boxcar was strange and unfamiliar. And frightening, as were the smells and the glimpse of overcast sky through the open car door.

He stood over her and the blue glow of his eyes brought it all back.

He was the monster again—the monster the voices had made him.

Get away from me, his mind told her. *Get away from Haversham.*

And with that he turned, the power rising up in him, his eyes starting to squint from the headache, and jumped through the open boxcar door.

All she could do was stand there and sob.

Chapter Twelve

1

Biff and Buffy, the mayor's children, were dispatched to school early, sent by cab instead of school bus. This was done by Elliot himself. Irna, his wife, was in the bedroom, the door closed.

Biff and Buffy wanted to see their mother, of course, but she wouldn't let them, which caused them to exchange supsicious glances and look balefully up at their father.

He shooed them out the door to the waiting cab and said, "Don't worry about your mother. She just has a headache."

Which was, in fact, true.

When he'd been wrestling around with her on the floor back at Emma's house, she'd accidentally struck her head, and she now possessed a goose egg the size of a golf ball on one side of it.

Elliot went into the bathroom to check the

scratches on his face. There was a council meeting within an hour and a half. It wouldn't do to have the mayor show up looking like he'd just spent the night in a cat house.

For a moment he was ashamed of something else he saw in the mirror, too. Despite the seriousness of the situation—Emma would probably never speak to him again, Irna was going to leave him, for sure— there was in his eyes the unmistakable sparkle of pride.

Yes, pride.

Elliot, however temporarily, had broken his chains, and it felt good, like a prisoner who'd escaped from a life sentence. He might be captured again, but at least he would have sweet memories of the time he was free. He had enjoyed the sex, the flattery Emma had showered on him, the sense that at his age, in his wife-captured position, he could still feel powerful in an erotic way. He had never been a Don Juan, true, but before he'd met Irna he had not exactly been celibate, either.

Then the sparkle died in his gaze as he remembered what Irna had looked like once their wrestling on Emma's floor had ceased.

She had stopped screaming, stopped hitting and kicking out, and her face had caused him to drop his hands at his side.

He had once seen a woman whose husband had died in an auto accident while she sat in the seat across from him—the woman had gone berserk. The ambulance attendants had had to chase her through a field, tackle her to bring her back. Elliot had never forgotten the shock and grief in her eyes—surely

Christ's eyes had borne this same misery—and so he had been shocked when he had seen the same grief in his wife's eyes on the floor of Emma's bathroom that morning. He could not quite forget her expression, nor his realization that there was something in his wife he did not know. For too many years she had been his jailer and his boss—worried about his career, his choice of friends, even the style of clothes he wore. So he had assumed that she was, at heart, as indifferent to him as he was to her.

Yet obviously she wasn't, as her eyes had told him in their terrible way.

He stood in just his trousers, his face lathered with Zest, his mouth hanging open in a dumb little circle—a kind of amazement, he supposed, because he had not expected Irna's reaction at all.

Oh, he could well imagine her following him (which she had, suspicious that he was "going back to the office," which he rarely did) and he could even imagine her, in her possessive way, breaking into Emma's and embarrassing them both.

But he certainly could not have predicted that look in her eyes. That look of disappointment and heartbreak that lingered with him.

In some awful way he'd been wrong about her, and he did not care for the feeling at all.

In the back of his closet he kept the neckties his father had worn, which Elliot had collected the day of his dad's death.

He wore them only on special occasions. He had decided, following the events at Emma's to turn this

271

into a special occasion, indeed.

He selected a wine-colored Wembley. He could remember his father wearing it. Always with a white shirt. Always tied in a Windsor. His father was one of those lucky men who could look dapper wearing a blue work shirt.

Finished dressing, he went to the bedroom door, listened intently. He heard her slow, steady breathing and assumed she was sleeping.

The familiar chime of the grandfather clock rang pleasantly throughout the house.

Then she coughed. Faintly. But just enough to indicate that she was probably awake.

He eased the door open and peeked in.

And couldn't believe what he saw.

She sat stark naked on the edge of the bed—she had retained her high school cheerleader's body even after all these years—and in her hands was an instrument he recognized as the handgun he sometimes practiced with at the police station in an effort to show the cops that, as a mayor, he was sympathetic to their cause.

Without thinking, he ran across the bedroom and ripped the weapon from her hands.

When she looked up at him, the same expression she'd worn at Emma's was on her face again.

He stood silent for a long moment, the overcast day pressing at the window, an array of perfumes from her dressing table filling his nostrils, a pair of his dirty socks sticking out from under the lid of the clothes hamper—and then he said, "I don't want you to hurt yourself, Irna."

"I shouldn't have gone over there," she said. He could see—and hear—that she was cried out. Now

272

her voice was hollow.

He started to put his hand on her shoulder. Withdrew it. True, they made love occasionally, but any intimacy, any tenderness was long gone. Even the prospect of it embarrassed him.

"It's all right," he said.

She didn't seem to hear him. Indeed, seemed instead to be speaking to herself. "I've ruined our marriage, and I mean it. I shouldn't ever have forced you to kowtow to Raymond Stockbridge. I can see it made you miserable."

Softly, he said, "That's all going to change, this morning."

But again she didn't seem to be listening. "I just wanted us to be successful . . . the way my father never was."

Then the tears came.

She sat there naked, sobbing, and as he watched her something he had assumed was dead rekindled in his heart.

Some feeling that was part love and part pity—not a condescending pity but one that was simply the recognition of another human's grief—stirred him.

He sat next to her, and after a few times he managed to do what he'd been unable to do for so many years—slide his arm around her and hold her with fondness and genuine care.

She came into his embrace like a child lost in the vast cruelty of existence and badly in need of comfort. And then he surprised himself even more by joining her tears with his own—though he had no exact idea why he was crying, just some sense of loss, some sense of failure, some odd sense now of renewal.

Finally, when she was cried out, when her breathing became heavier, as if she were going to sleep right there in his arms, Elliot said, in his arch, uncomfortable manner, "You know, there's still a good possibility that I love you."

Her head threw back and he couldn't be sure exactly what escaped her lips—half-sob, half-laugh. Whatever, it imbued her eyes with a great fondness, and she threw her arms around him with childish glee. "You're such a nerd sometimes, the way you talk, Elliot, and that's one thing I've always loved about you."

He supposed, under the circumstances, that what she'd just said was a compliment.

He got in the spirit of the moment and gave his wife the kind of kiss he hadn't—even in the throes of passion—given to Emma last night.

Somewhere during all this, Irna's hand found his hard, needful sex and lay gently back on their marriage bed to take him inside.

Thirty-five minutes later Elliot left his house, walking with the kind of purposeful stride he didn't exhibit often.

He had decided to walk to City Hall.

He still needed time to think out what he was going to do, say.

How he was going to help the Stockbridge empire crumble to so much dust and ash.

2

Sometimes the roaring got so bad in his ears that Brian Courtney had to stop and slam his hands against his head in a futile attempt to stop the noise.

That was one way he knew they were in control again—the roaring, and the feverish feeling that alternated with chills. When the chills took him over he lost his sight and was guided by some consciousness beyond his own powers.

Davie Mason.

During his days below the surface of the ice, he had discovered many things, not least of which was that Davie Mason had changed. Not that he could see Davie, of course, but his former friend was a strong presence, thanks to the way he could speak words directly into Brian's mind.

Brian trudged on.

He was just rounding the corner of a slum section of Haversham.

In the gray morning a garbage truck pushed along the curb. Two black men with gold teeth and doomed eyes picked up waiting garbage cans with an air of misery and hopelessness.

They looked up suddenly as Brian approached them.

For just a moment he read their minds—saw the failure that was their lot, and what it did to them—

and wished he could help them in some way. They stood less of a chance than even orphans did.

They did not respond in kind. Rather, his presence seemed to unnerve them. One of the men banged on the door of the truck cab and signaled for the driver to take off. The driver, staring at Brian through the windshield, must have sensed what his compatriots did. He pushed the twelve-speed into gear so quickly, he ground a pound of metal doing so.

Don't waste your time on unfortunates, said the voice in his mind.

Davie Mason's voice.

You know what you must do.

The Continental sat in the sweeping drive of a colonial-style mansion.

During bike trips from the orphanage, Brian had often passed this place and wondered what it would be like to live here. The people inside probably never worried about money or sickness or loneliness. He sensed that they were a breed apart—like aliens that stepped down from flying saucers.

Today his impression was different.

Destroy them.

By this time the intensity of the voice was overwhelming.

In the bitter-cold morning, Brian fell to his knees next to a stout fir tree. Pressed his hands to his head. Tried to rid his mind of Davie's commands.

Hail Mary—

What had the priest told him once? That if you could block out all other thoughts, let the Virgin fill your mind entirely, she would grant you any wish you desired.

Which was what he tried to do.

Concentrated so hard that at first he felt Davie's thoughts begin to recede like water withdrawing from a pool

Hail Mary . . .

Yes, it was working.

He wanted to help Davie, to avenge the terrible things that had been done to him and to the other kids who had been hurled into the chemical spill after being murdered—

Yes, he wanted to help.

But Davie wanted vengeance so badly that he seemed as insane as the people he hated.

And that was what frightened Brian—Davie's hatred, and his desire to wipe out the whole of Haversham.

He had to fight that command in his head.

Hail Mary—

Brian's breathing began to smooth out, the chill-and-fevers sensation to withdraw from his body, his mind becoming truly his own again.

Hail Mary—

She was taking over.

With good thoughts—

And then—

Destroy them, Brian. All of them.

Brian fell to the ground and began to twist, keeping his ears covered the whole time.

In his thoughts, he pleaded with Davie: *This isn't the way. Too many innocent people will die.*

But Davie's angry presence filled him, nonetheless.

Brian got to his feet. He reached out into the air as if to touch somebody—he thought of the woman in the photograph, the woman he'd pretended was his mother. *Help me.*

Dimly, he could hear her, far back in his mind, humming a gentle tune, and he let his would-be mother come through as loudly as she could, as if he were tuning in a radio station a great distance away.

Davie fought him the whole time.

But finally the woman's voice became loud enough to drown out Davie—and for a time hatred ebbed in Brian's soul. He let his eyes close and let her beautiful singing fill his ears.

He wanted to run, far away, through the hills so that nobody but Caroline could find him—run with the woman's singing drowning out all else.

Then, abruptly, a headache far worse than any he'd yet known seized him.

When he opened his eyes again the beautiful singing was gone and there was death in his gaze.

On his feet again, Brian now moved toward the Continental. First he destroyed the front door of the car. Metal and glass and rubber melted like so much plastic. Within seconds the entire car raged with flames.

Brian stood off to the side, watching an older couple in the black attire of servant and maid rush down the steps of the mansion. They looked at him and screamed. Brian cut through the massive wooden pillars that held up the porch. The roof caved in, crashing to the ground.

Now the servants were joined by the owners of the home. The husband clutched a rifle. Brian looked at it in contempt. The weapon began to glow with such heat that the man threw it down, cursing.

The air was filled with the rancid odor of smoke.

Brian walked away, back toward town.

People edged away from him.

Brian was filled with a triumphant sense of power and his ears rang with the sound of children's laughter.

3

A chunky woman wearing a faded housedress and heavy black oxfords finished her dusting of the council chambers just as Mayor Elliot Hughes banged the meeting to session.

The woman, startled by the gavel, glanced up as if somebody had been shot.

Then she picked up her rag and left.

Around the U-shaped table sat the entire council.

Seated in the chairs in the center were Diane Baines and John Tyler.

"These people have asked to present a case to us, and I have granted them permission to do so," Elliot said abruptly.

Just as Hughes finished speaking, the rear door opened up and a massive figure loomed on the threshold. Raymond Stockbridge.

He entered the room with such formidable difficulty that it was almost impressive. Dressed, as usual, in black, and in his capelike cloak, he went to one of the back pews and seated himself with sudden grace.

"Proceed," his voice boomed. "If I don't like what I hear, I'll let you know about it."

Diane had been feeling strong and hopeful—until now. The presence of Stockbridge ended her positive mood. He was like an evil uncle who abruptly showed up to spoil a birthday party.

Tyler seemed less swayed by the huge man's entrance.

He turned to the mayor and said, "I don't think Gus Fenster's death the other night was an accident."

The six council members were accustomed to uneventful and rubber-stamp meetings. They generally knew how the Stockbridge family wanted them to vote, and so it took no effort on their part to sit there, listen to arguments pro and con, and then simply cast their ballots in the preordained way. City hall business was conducted just like this in hundreds of American cities that, if not run by men as evil as Stockbridge, were nonetheless run by bullying mayors and political cabals.

Diane almost smiled at their consternation. They looked at the mayor and then they looked at each other and then they looked back at Stockbridge.

Mr. Sale, the man whom Stockbridge had made a millionaire several times over, cleared his throat and said, "We've got too much other business to bother with something like this."

Stockbridge smiled.

Obviously his people were going to come through, squelch the investigation before it began.

The mayor raised and lowered his gavel once again.

"Proceed," he said to Tyler.

Tyler turned back to the council. A very tired-looking Samuel Coffey nodded for him to go ahead.

"Gus Fenster called me the day he died and said that he had proof that the stairs at Windhaven—the stairs that were supposedly in bad repair—were in good condition and that the Mason boy could not have fallen to his death because of them. He was going to elaborate on his statement for me, but before I could get out there he'd died in the fire."

"What are you saying, Mr. Tyler?" Coffey asked him, to the great displeasure of the other council members.

"That Gus Fenster was murdered."

The door in the rear of the chamber opened again. This time it was Mrs. Kilrane who entered. She looked much less severe today, thanks to a white turtleneck sweater, a blue blazer, and a flattering amount of makeup.

She slipped into the pew next to her father, whispered a few words to him, and then stood up. "I would like to address the council, if I may."

She made her voice as sweet as a country naïf's. But her glare told her real feelings. Her eyes seemed to shoot lasers of hatred directly at the mayor, a man who had obviously let her down.

"I have just returned from the county attorney's office," Mrs. Kilrane said, approaching the front of the chamber. She waved an official-looking document at the mayor. "He has decided to indict Diane Baines for possession of a controlled substance." She shook her head toward the council members. "Now, I'd hardly think you'd want a woman like her addressing this council."

"I agree," Sale said, with an eagerness that was almost embarrassing. "And I'd say that also goes for Tyler here, too."

The other members nodded in quick agreement, obviously concerned about the direction their meeting had been taking.

Diane stood up and faced Mrs. Kilrane. "You know what's been going on in this town for the past fifteen years—maybe longer. Children at the orphanage have been dying—and this community has a right to know why."

For the first time that morning, Stockbridge's face reflected concern.

He looked at his daughter. She shook her head, telling him to say nothing.

"And you are accusing the orphanage of some complicity in their deaths, I suppose?" Mrs. Kilrane said.

"Yes, I am," Diane said.

"This is outrageous," Sale said in his most commanding voice. His glance at the other members demanded that they back him up. Like bad actors in a crowd scene, their voices were added, loudly and theatrically, to the hubbub.

In the middle of all this, the east door opened and Caroline Hayes walked in.

Diane's first impression was that the girl had been injured somehow—her face was dirty and her clothes scruffy. Diane's impulse was to go over to her and hug her protectively. And Caroline obviously had the same impulse because she ran across the council chambers straight into Diane's arms and clung to the older woman as if a demon were trying to snatch her.

"It's all right, it's all right," Diane soothed.

She was soon joined by Tyler, who stroked the girl's hair. From it he picked pieces of weeds and straw. Caroline looked as if she'd spent the night in a ditch.

"Is this touching scene really necessary?" Sale said witheringly.

"Give them a few minutes," the mayor said. He obviously knew better than to look to the back of the room, where Mrs. Kilrane and her father were fuming.

Caroline kept up her sobbing. She was crying so hard that her slender body flung itself against Diane

To the mayor, Diane said, "May we take her out in the hall a few moments?"

The mayor, still avoiding eye contact with the Stockbridge contingent in the rear, nodded. "I don't see why not."

"What the hell is this, a nursery school?" one of the other council members demanded.

"Come on, honey," Diane soothed, taking the girl out of the chambers.

The hall was marble, a remnant from the days when such buildings imitated Roman architecture. The ceiling looked to be thirty feet high. Ornate cornices swelled like frosting on a cake. A broad, sweeping staircase disappeared into the gray light above.

"Calm down, honey, it'll be all right."

"But I'm scared for Brian," Caroline sobbed.

"Brian's dead," Diane said.

"No, he's not. I saw him."

Diane and Tyler looked at each other.

"Where did you see him?" Diane asked.

Caroline told them. All of it. Brian leading her from the house. Brian taking her to the trainyard. Brian possessed by the evil spirits of the children in the swamp.

"They want him to wipe out Haversham, kill everybody in it."

Diane watched Caroline with a terrible feeling that the girl had come unhinged sometime during the night. She got down on one knee, holding the girl tenderly, putting her face close to Caroline's. The girl smelled of mud and tears.

"This has all been very stressful for you," Diane said.

Caroline shook her head. "I really did see Brian, and the children really do want him to destroy Haversham."

Now Tyler got down on one knee. "Hon, sometimes we think things so vividly they become real—even when they're not. You see?"

Diane was about to take over again when she heard the sound of crashing glass and the screams of several men in the council chambers.

She and Tyler raced back into the room just in time to see the tall leaded windows smashing out in gale winds.

Their eyes fastened on the small figure that was causing the winds—Brian.

This time the headache was different. It was as if the pain had taken control of his entire body.

Brian looked at the cowering, corrupt people before him and saw them as Davie saw them—as scum, dishonest, disloyal, treacherous. This was what humankind was really like—a selfish, gossiping, prejudiced bunch of petty little people with petty little dreams.

285

They deserved to die.

And in Brian now rose that desire—to kill them, to watch eyeballs burst open, to watch limbs being ripped off, to watch blood flow until it covered the floors and people had to wade in it. Only their screams could sate him, only their suffering could ease his pain.

He did not even mind the pain of the headache now, indeed he seemed to revel in it, as if it were the source of a special secret enjoyment.

Diane grabbed Caroline just as the young girl reached for Brian.

Several people lay on the floor, twisted and disfigured. Intermingled with the smell of fire was the reek of blood. The council chambers was becoming a killing floor.

Diane grabbed Caroline and, with Tyler, ducked behind a massive desk.

Sirens erupted in the distance as the ceiling caved in and the screaming became louder. It was worse than screaming—it was the pleading of suffering people.

After a silence of some seconds, Diane looked around the corner of the desk and saw Brian. He stood completely still. The pain that had shone on his face before seemed to be subsiding. He looked around the chambers, as if he could make no more sense of the destruction than Diane could.

He backed away, then turned and ran, his slapping feet echoing down what was left of the corridor.

By midafternoon, Mrs. Kilrane had deputized virtually every man in Haversham who could tote a gun.

The downtown area of the town looked like an army depot. Weapons of every description were being loaded onto the backs of jeeps. Men in field gear lounged around sidewalks with an air of purpose and pleasure. It was not often that the law allowed you to hunt a real human being.

Diane and Tyler watched all this as their car moved slowly through the streets of the loop.

Caroline was in the back seat, exhausted from the events of the past few days.

Tyler said, "I'm going to have you let me off up the street."

"At the biker's bar?"

He nodded.

"I wish you wouldn't," she said. "Not without some kind of backup." She smiled. "You could always ask me to go along, you know."

For a time he said nothing, did not seem to have heard her at all. He watched the streets. Haversham definitely resembled a town at war, some small European town during World War II, awaiting invasion.

Finally, he said, after checking in the back seat to

make sure that Caroline was still asleep, "They're going to kill him when they find him."

"I know." Then Diane paused. "But if we can find him first, that won't happen."

"That's why I want to see my good old friend Merle."

"Why?"

"He knows something. I'm not sure what, I'm not even sure it will be useful, but I've got to try."

With that he pulled the car up in front of the biker tavern that Merle owned. He glanced in the back. Touched Caroline's leg.

"She finally looks like she's getting some decent sleep," he said.

Diane nodded. "That's something we could all use, I guess."

Tyler smiled. "We will, soon enough." He leaned over and kissed her. "See you soon."

"I'll be happy to wait."

"Take Caroline home. Let her sleep in a bed for a while."

"You're a damn good man, you know that?"

"Careful," he smiled. "You may just get me to believe that someday."

He got out of the car, the cold swimming like wraiths into the interior of the vehicle. He nodded and went up to the front of the place.

Several bikes were angled around the door like a trap in an obstacle course.

He waved and went on inside.

Tyler was greeted by the glares of several middle-aged men doing their best to look fierce in straggly hair, leather vests decorated with swastikas, and jeans that looked greasy enough to serve as a floor in a car repair shop.

A few of them set down their mugs of beer and turned themselves his way, as if they were going to attack him.

Tyler kept walking toward the door that led to the stairway.

"Hey, asshole," the bartender called after him. "You musta forgot what happened to you last time you was here."

Tyler remained silent and kept walking.

"Hey, fuck face, you hear me or what?" the bartender said again.

By now he was almost to the door—was, in fact, reaching out a hand to take the knob.

The biker dressed up like a Viking picked up a pool cue and ran screaming across the tavern to Tyler.

Obviously the biker, who wielded the cue with the skill of a practiced hand, was ready to open up Tyler's head like a watermelon cleaved with an axe.

But then Tyler surprised him.

The ex-sheriff spun around and whipped from his jacket, in an easy, almost invisible motion, a Magnum big enough to put a hole in the side of an armored truck.

The tavern, which had been alive with the noise of the jukebox and cursing, fell suddenly silent.

There was just the Viking's face and the huge Magnum pushing into that face.

"You have any idea what this punk is going to

look like if I pull the trigger?" Tyler asked.

Nobody said anything.

"Just so we understand each other," Tyler said.

He wrenched the big man around, slammed him into the door. Then he pushed him into a heap across a table that gave way beneath the Viking's weight.

Tyler glared at the bikers, who had the good sense to go back to their beers.

Then he went upstairs in search of Merle.

You could feel it everywhere. The tension. The terror.

Word of Brian Courtney's mysterious and deadly powers had obviously made its way throughout Haversham.

No children played on the streets. Patrol cars cruised slowly down alleys. Worried citizens stood on street corners, talking and watching. Especially watching.

Diane saw all this as she made her way home from the biker bar.

She was caught up in her fears for Tyler (could she really be this deeply in love in so short a time?) and her fears for Brian. She did not like to think what would happen to Caroline's mind if harm came to Brian. But even if they managed to find him before Stockbridge's forces did, what could they do with him? What was the source of his powers? He had been possessed by some kind of demonic force—and how could they help him?

She was thinking this when a car pulled abruptly in front of her.

She slammed on the brakes, hearing Caroline cry out from the back seat and her own curses beneath her breath.

She looked up just in time to see Farnsworth jumping from his official sheriff's vehicle, the one that had been "hers" just a few days earlier.

He was dressed by the book, as always, a crease in his pants, a shine on his gold buttons, his hair just the right length. There was only one thing wrong about his appearance. His face. You'd think that a lawman who followed the rules as carefully as he did would look much happier.

"I need to talk to you," he said. "Sorry if I scared you."

In the back seat, Caroline was rubbing her eyes. Coming awake.

"You picked a hell of a way to stop me," Diane said.

"You wouldn't have had to hit your brakes if you'd been paying attention to the road," he said.

Looking over the relative positions of their cars, she could see that he was right.

"Okay, fine, so give me a ticket."

He looked pained. "Diane, God, listen I—"

"You're sorry." Her voice was almost mocking.

"Yes, I am."

"Sheriffs don't have to be sorry. They've got their badges to protect them."

"Diane, I didn't ask for this job."

"Right."

She could contain her anger no longer. "I really thought we were friends."

He said it. Simply. Without melodrama or fuss.

"They're blackmailing me. Isn't that one of the two ways the Stockbridge family prefers to deal with people—either pay them off outright or find some kind of hold on them?"

He then went on to explain what had happened years earlier and how the Stockbridges had seen fit to hold it against him. And how they had used their knowledge to get him to become sheriff after the drugs were planted in her home.

"I just wanted to apologize."

"Well, thank you," she said.

She felt sorry for him, but she hadn't forgiven him. Couldn't. Not yet.

"I'm cold," Caroline said.

Diane had the front window open.

"I've got to be going."

"I have to ask you a question," he said. "Do you have any idea where Brian Courtney might be?"

"No! Don't tell him!" Caroline exploded. She sat up in the seat. "Please, don't tell him!"

Diane frowned. "You may not believe this, but I don't have the slightest idea where he is."

"I don't have to tell you how dangerous he is."

"He isn't dangerous!" Caroline cried out. "He isn't!"

The sheriff turned to Caroline. "Do you know where he is?"

She sank back.

"She was with us in the city council chambers when Brian was there. That's the last any of us saw of him."

"I didn't ask you, I asked her."

"She doesn't know."

"Do you know, little girl?" the sheriff asked, leaning into the back seat.

Caroline shook her head no.

The sheriff stared at her for long moments, then returned his attention to Diane.

"For all our sakes, he's got to be found."

"I suppose he does, yes."

"Damn," the sheriff said, looking at her with a mixture of affection and anger. "You never let me get close to you for one minute, did you? You're like a stranger."

She could sense the tears in his voice, see how his eyes were getting watery.

He turned and stormed back to his car.

She just sat there stunned and depressed.

Tyler couldn't believe it.

There in front of a TV set in the dumpy apartment, whirling around on a VCR that fed the screen, was the Jane Fonda exercise tape.

And there in front of the TV was Merle the biker, doing exercises.

It was like watching an elephant trying out ballet.

Merle looked as if he didn't know whether to be angry or embarrassed about Tyler's sudden appearance.

Before Merle could do anything, Tyler moved across the room, lowered the Magnum at Merle's estimable belly, and said, "Slimming down for a big party?"

"Fuck yourself."

He waved the Magnum at Merle again. "I want to

293

know everything your cousin told you about Mrs. Kilrane and her father."

"Tough shit. I don't have to tell you anything."

Jane Fonda was telling her home audience how important it was to exercise regularly when Tyler decided to prove to Merle what a tough sumbitch he was.

Tyler put a Magnum slug dead through the TV screen.

It didn't take long for Merle to get down to some serious talking. He began by relating a most peculiar story: how Mrs. Kilrane had killed her brother and her father found out and forced her to live in the underground room. But as Mrs. Kilrane grew up, she got stronger and took her revenge on her mentally unstable father by convincing him that *he'd* been killing little boys all along.

Tyler listened to it all, alternately fascinated and sickened.

Chapter Thirteen

1

By three that afternoon the sky was so dark it was virtually dusk already.

Mrs. Kilrane ordered that the orphanage children be fed early so that they could be put to bed early.

Brian Courtney had not been found and Mrs. Kilrane expected a night of trouble. She sat now behind her desk staring out her window at the swamp across from the orphanage. The place now held some fascination for her that it never had before.

After a time she rose up from her chair and crossed to the window.

She could not believe what she thought she'd just seen in the marshy area.

A kind of glowing blue color.

Impossible.

She was ready to go get her binoculars when there was a knock on her door.

Angrily, she went to answer it, threw open the door, and confronted the man who stood there.

Her father.

Her pathetic father.

He held something up to her.

When she saw what it was, she felt disgusted. She slapped it from his hand.

"They want me," he blubbered. Apparently he had been crying for some time.

"They want me," he repeated.

"Who wants you?" she snapped.

"Them," he said, nodding to the swamp. "The children."

She thought of the council chambers this morning. Brian Courtney. The terrible firestorm and windstorm he'd set off.

"And they're going to get me," he wailed. "They're going to get me."

For once, she had to agree with him. Whatever was going on in Haversham, it was obviously aimed at the Stockbridge family.

It was time to call Dodge and implement her plan.

2

Brian waited until the sky turned an ugly and threatening black before climbing out of the drainage ditch where he'd been hiding since leaving the council chambers that morning.

He took gravel roads, guided by some kind of blind instinct, running in and out of gullies, passing through the edges of woods, climbing fences and running through acre after acre of corn trampled by the winter weather.

Where was he going?

He couldn't be sure.

All he knew was that Davie was in control again, which accounted for the blinding headache and the chills up and down his body.

But he plunged on anyway.

Once he encountered a pheasant lifting to the sky from a blind. The sight of the bird struck Brian as beautiful. He wished his life were his own again.

The name of the place was the Dekker farm. Brian had played in it several times. There was a great barn to hide in for cowboy-and-Indian shootouts. The people at the orphanage did not like the idea of the kids coming all the way out here, of course, but Brian and Davie Mason had snuck away every chance they'd gotten.

Now, in the dying daylight, there was something ominous about the deserted buildings and fallow fields.

Brian stood shivering in the crowding darkness, wondering why the children had wished him to come out here.

He moved forward.

The car in the driveway stopped him.

Whose car?

He moved forward more carefully, sneaking around the car, around the house, and up to the barn itself.

At first he heard nothing but the ancient creaking wood of the place, a distant dog, an even more distant train. Then he heard the voices, and at first the sound almost shocked his ears.

Voices in the barn.

Where could they be coming from?

He stopped, fell against the barn door. His breath came raggedly. He was soaked with sweat. Why did the children want him to be here, on this farm? And what did his mission have to do with the voices below?

Against his will, he came away from the door and walked to the center of the barn.

Then he saw it.

The trapdoor leading downstairs.

In all the time he'd played out here, he'd never once guessed that there had been a door like this. The idea of it both excited and terrified him.

He got down on his hands and knees and crawled over to the trapdoor and looked down.

He could see a flashlight play off the walls below and hear the voices even more clearly.

That was when he lost his balance and fell straight down into the hole the trapdoor had been hiding.

His screams sounded like reverberations inside a tin can.

Dodge waited until he saw the bedroom light go off before he moved on Diane Baines's house.

The kid would be sleepy, which would make things easier.

Dodge moved.

He ran up the small sidewalk, straight up to the door, and kicked it in with a single crash of his combat boot.

Diane Baines (and man, was she a foxy-looking lady) was standing in the center of the living room. She was just about to open her pretty mouth in protest when Dodge brought the rifle clean across her face, knocking her out in a heap on the floor.

The rest was simple.

When he heard the screaming, Tyler looked up and saw a small boy's body tumbling down through the air.

He reached the body just in time to break the fall and place the boy gently on the ground. A quick look at the kid's face revealed the biggest surprise of all.

The boy was Brian Courtney.

Behind Tyler, the sullen voice of Merle said, "Ain't that the kid everybody's looking for?"

"Yeah. But don't get any ideas about turning him in." He brought the Magnum up in plain sight so that the biker wouldn't do anything dumb.

Then he turned his attention back to Brian.

"You all right?"

"I—I think so. What're you doing down here?"

Tyler nodded back to Merle. "He was just explaining to me who really killed all the children over the years."

"Mr. Stockbridge?" Brian asked.

"No," Tyler said. "That's the surprising thing. It wasn't Raymond Stockbridge at all."

The surface of the swampy area danced with frightening blue light, the chemical-infested waters below boiling up through refuse and ice alike.

People driving past pointed to it but continued quickly on their way. Too many strange things were happening in Haversham. They wanted only the peace and comfort of their homes.

Mrs. Kilrane was looking down on the swampy area from the window in her study when Dodge came through the door with Diane Baines and Caroline Hayes.

Mrs. Kilrane turned from the window. "Before you say anything, Diane, understand that I could easily have you charged with kidnapping."

Diane started to protest, but Mrs. Kilrane raised her hand. "Technically, Caroline is still a charge of this institution. You have no right to take her as you have."

This time, Diane did speak. "Your father has been killing children for more than twenty years. And we have proof of that now."

Mrs. Kilrane smiled chillingly. "Proof?"

"Yes, Brian Courtney's word, for one."

"Very impressive." Mrs. Kilrane seemed to enjoy her sarcasm. Then the smile vanished. "He's coming to get my father, isn't he?"

"Brian?"

"Yes."

"I assume he is, yes."

"Well, isn't he going to be surprised when he tries to destroy us to find that you've joined us. I don't think he'll do anything foolish then, do you?"

At last the whole scheme seemed to make sense to Diane.

Terrible sense.

Caroline started crying. Diane hugged her tightly.

"You don't want a ride back to town?"

"No fuckin' way, man," Merle said.

Brian spooked the biker. Terrified him. As if the boy had some terrible plague.

Merle, once he'd divested himself of all useful information concerning his cousin and Mrs. Kilrane, went up the ladder as quickly as Tyler would let him.

"It's a long walk," Tyler said.

"I'm healthy," Merle said. The three-hundred pound man saw no irony in his words.

"Up to you," Tyler said.

Merle took another disgusted—and frightened—look at Brian and set off walking into the gloom that touched the surrounding farm fields. A cold, full moon shone on the frosty terrain below.

"Come on," Tyler said.

They walked away from the barn to where Tyler's car was parked. Tyler had forced Merle to drive him over to Tyler's on his bike, where they'd picked up the ex-sheriff's car.

The interior smelled of cigarette smoke and seat leather.

Tyler started the heater right away. Brian hugged the passenger's side of the seat, leaning his head against the door. It was easy to see that the boy was in bad need of medical attention in addition to needing sleep and food.

Tyler drove out of the farmyard. They soon passed Merle crunching across a field. Honked at him. He waved back, dismally.

The night was beautiful to Tyler. The black stands of trees against the hills. The moonlight on snowy pines. The silver clouds against the black sky. Beautiful. Ideal.

Across the seat from him Brian seemed to be almost dozing. Tyler thought about all the women in his life. Somehow none of the relationships had ever led to the birth of a child. His child. He'd always wanted one, had promised himself that there would be one when the right woman came along, but then booze and self-pity and a life of drifting had managed to rule out the possibility of that life.

He was thinking about this, forgetting about the road, when the rear wheels slipped on some ice and jarred him out of his reverie.

He looked over at Brian to see how the kid was doing.

The hair literally stood up along the back of Tyler's neck.

Brian glowed blue. And his eyes were coils of madness and power that Tyler did not even want to contemplate.

"Get out of the car," Brian said.

His voice was slowed down.

Not his own.

Tyler knew better than to argue with him. He stopped the car near a DX station, just inside Haversham.

"Get out," Brian said.

What was he going to do? Tyler wondered.

But he got out.

"Brian," he said, "listen to me. I don't think you've

killed anybody so far. Now that we know who is the real killer, now you don't have to kill anybody. Do you understand me?''

Brian pulled the door closed, moved over on the seat and drove off.

A twelve-year-old boy.

Driving.

Tyler did the only thing he could. He ran after the car in the night, shouting the boy's name.

Dodge marched them up the stairs to the attic and then closed and bolted the door behind them.

It was ten minutes before Diane, huddled in the corner with Caroline, heard the breathing.

At first she thought it might be just some manifestation of steam heat.

Some hissing sound.

But then she listened very carefully and found that the source was human.

Moonlight graced the silhouettes of boxes and dress forms and old toys that cluttered the attic. The silver light lent the things a touch of magic they did not deserve. Even the cobwebs looked silver and graceful in the light.

Diane and Caroline searched through all this and then found him.

Raymond Stockbridge.

Hiding in the corner.

In the shadows, his eyes were two pathetic insane slits.

The first thing he said to them was, "Do you want to be my friend?"

Diane and Caroline were too shocked to speak. They had no idea why Mrs. Kilrane had had Dodge bring them up here. To be with her father?

"Do you want to be my friend?" Stockbridge

repeated in his singsong voice again.

This was the most powerful man in Haversham?

"I'll give you a present," he said.

His fat hand reached with something.

Diane, reluctantly, put out her own hand. Took it.

The cold metal of a toy soldier now lay in the palm of her hand.

"I give them to all my friends. It makes my daughter mad when I do it. But I don't mean any harm by it."

He sounded almost as if he were going to cry.

"When they give me the shock treatments, they won't let me take my soldiers in with me. They make me leave them in my room."

"God, what's wrong with him?" Caroline sobbed.

But Diane realized there was no way she could explain to the girl what the trouble was here. That Raymond Stockbridge was totally insane—that Raymond Stockbridge had probably killed many children.

"I gave her brother one of these," Stockbridge went on. "The day he died, I gave him one of these." In the shadows, his blubbering face took on an almost comic look. He was hopelessly mad. "Lavonne doesn't think I know, but I do . . . she pushed him on purpose and that's why he died. On purpose. That's the truth."

Then he started sobbing, much as Caroline had done earlier.

At first Diane felt revulsion. All she could think of was how powerful this man had been. How much pain and agony he had brought to other people. But finally she could not deny her own humanity by denying Stockbridge his—as he lay there shaking in his misery, she put out her hand and touched him.

And incredibly, that stopped his weeping.

When he brought his face up from his sleeve this time, the crazed look was gone from his eyes. He said, quite soberly, "She's kept me this way for years. But you probably didn't know that, did you?"

"Kept you what way?"

"Drugged up. Having electro-shock treatment. Using me when it suited her needs—keeping me up here when it didn't."

All Diane could do was stare at him.

The transition from helpless insanity to sober reality shocked her. She knew this was not uncommon in several forms of severe mental illness. But was Stockbridge mentally ill or only, as he suggested, a pawn of his daughter?

But she didn't have time to wonder anymore, because a rear panel opened in the back of the attic, and silhouetted against the light were the shapes of Mrs. Kilrane and Ken Dodge.

Dodge still toted his rifle.

"It's time," Mrs. Kilrane said.

Dodge came over and led them back to the secret panel that opened on a staircase.

Diane had a terrible premonition of where they were going.

6

Diane, Caroline, and Raymond Stockbridge were led from the back of the orphanage up the hill to the edge of the swamp.

Dodge kept his gun trained carefully on them.

The bitter cold revived Diane's anger at Mrs. Kilrane. She now wondered if the woman's father weren't somehow a victim—just as the children had been.

When they got to the fencing, Dodge held the wire apart so they could climb through.

"It's all over for you, whether you understand that or not," Diane said to Mrs. Kilrane.

"I appreciate the advice."

"Too many people know."

"Around here, people know what we tell them to know. And nothing more. Now hurry up."

"You killed Davie Mason, didn't you?" Caroline said.

Mrs. Kilrane reached out with a swift hand and smacked her hard across the mouth.

Finally they reached the churning waters. The winter wind blew snow into their faces.

Mrs. Kilrane went up to her father.

"You first," she said.

Diane tried to read the old man's expression, but she couldn't. She imagined that he felt angry, betrayed, afraid—many things.

"She's right," he said. "Diane is right. They'll know it was you and what you did."

"What I did to my brother?" she smirked. "Or what I did to all those children—the ones you thought you killed?"

Diane was surprised to see that Stockbridge's face remained inscrutable.

"Oh, if you and your mother had only been as smart as you'd thought. I knew who really killed those children—you did, because you were jealous of the attention I gave your brother. I was wrong there: I should have paid more attention to you. But I didn't, because I wanted to be close to my son, my heir. And that's why you killed all those little boys over the years—because for you they were your brother—and you wanted to kill him over and over again."

"You're having one of your lucid moments, Father," she smirked. "It's quite impressive, actually."

Then, without warning, she pushed him.

The huge man fell backward, his arms windmilling, his scream lost in the wind.

The glowing blue waters awaited him.

And then the voices came.

The million myriad tiny screams of children long denied their vengeance—finally offered their reward for their pain on earth and their purgatory below.

Stockbridge bobbed in the water momentarily, but even before he could sink, the tiny glowing hands of children began ripping his flesh from his bulk.

In no time his face was that of a skeleton.

"Oh, God!" Caroline shrieked. "Oh, God!"

7

As he pulled the big car into the Windhaven parking lot, Brian could hear the shouts of the rejoicing children in his mind.

He could also see the image of Raymond Stockbridge being ripped asunder—flesh and bone being torn into a human flotsam.

But he was not the person they wanted, of course.

Brian fled to the car and ran toward the swampy area.

Through the blowing snow he could see Caroline Hayes and Diane Baines standing by the edge of the swamp.

Power lashed out like an electric snake, cutting a tree in half, setting fire to grassy land around the swamp.

Then he saw Mrs. Kilrane.

She stood next to the swamp, too. Much as Brian wanted to destroy her himself, he knew that the dead children deserved her much more.

He ran faster toward the swampy area.

But then Mrs. Kilrane grabbed Caroline.

"If you come any closer, I'll throw her in," Mrs. Kilrane said.

Brian stopped running.

He hesitated on the outside of the fence surrounding the swamp.

"Let Dodge go get our car, and let us escape, and I won't harm Caroline," Mrs. Kilrane said.

Enraged as he was, eager to see her dead, Brian knew that he had no choice but to let Mrs. Kilrane have her way.

"You'd better do as she says," came a voice from behind him.

Tyler, panting, looking ready to collapse, came up behind him.

Brian looked up at him and nodded.

"All right," he said above the singing wind.

Mrs. Kilrane nodded to Dodge, who started toward Brian and Tyler.

And then he heard Diane scream.

From behind Mrs. Kilrane and Dodge came six glowing forms of children.

They crawled from the swamp, making noises that nearly deafened the ears.

Mrs. Kilrane and Dodge turned to look at them, and then to flee, but it was too late.

The hideous forms of children who had been thrown into the chemical muck, and whose forms were now little more than bones and wretched chunks of glowing meat, came for them.

Mrs. Kilrane turned to run, but Brian lunged for her and pushed her back to the edge of the swamp to where the children came.

"Brian, be careful!" Caroline screamed.

But it was too late. Brian threw all his weight against Mrs. Kilrane, and the two fell into the churning blue waters together.

For a few minutes the screams of Mrs. Kilrane could be heard even above the noises of the eating children as they passed her around like a meal.

Finally, she was nothing but bones.

The children sank back into the swamp. The waters gradually receded and became peaceful. A few moments later Brian's head appeared—hideous in a way because much of his face was gone now—but beautiful in the peacefulness of his gaze.

Then he sank out of sight.

8

"I'm glad you don't hate me," Sheriff Farnsworth
said outside the jail where Diane had gone to collect
the last of her things. The mayor stood next to
Farnsworth.

"No," Diane said, "I don't hate you."

Farnsworth said, "Friends?"

Diane smiled. "Friends." And she put out her hand
for him to shake, which he did.

"I guess it's really over, isn't it?" Diane asked.

"Yes. And with what we've found, there's no doubt
about what happened. Raymond Stockbridge knew
that his daughter killed her brother, and that she
killed other little boys at the orphanage, too, but by
the time he decided to do something about it, it was
too late. She had him committed, along with the help
of her mother, and kept him docile and dependent on
his drug addiction for the rest of his life. That was
she could control him. She gave him enough drugs
that he even got psychotic enough to wonder if he
hadn't killed all those little boys. But it was her. All
along." He shook his head. "She even killed her
husband, once he recognized her for what she was,
and kept his ashes in an urn in the attic."

Diane frowned. "The poor kids who died."

"From what was left of Mrs. Kilrane, I'd say they
had their vengeance."

314

"You going to stay around here?" Mayor Elliot Hughes asked.

Diane had never seen him look so self-confident before, and she had to admit that he seemed positively mayorly now that the yoke of the Stockbridge family had been lifted from his shoulders.

"Haversham is going to be like a brand new town," the mayor said.

Diane smiled. "I hope so."

Tyler and Caroline were waiting in the car when Diane got in and slid behind the wheel.

A rock song played. Tyler stared out the window, lost in his own thoughts, while in the back seat Caroline fiddled with something in her lap that Diane couldn't see.

"A burger and fries at Hardees sound good to anybody?" Diane asked.

Tyler shrugged. Caroline said nothing.

She wasn't going to impose any more artificial cheeriness on them or herself. A lot had happened in the past few days. It was going to take a long time to get over it. A quick lunch at Hardees was no miracle cure.

Haversham already looked different. There were people in the streets and small children on the sidewalks. As she drove, Diane turned off the radio. Nobody seemed to mind.

"Would you mind driving by the swamp?"

Diane and Tyler exchanged nervous glances.

"You sure you want to?" Diane asked.

"Yes, I am," Caroline said. "Sure, I mean."

Tyler sighed.

In ten minutes the car pulled up in front of the orphanage.

"Will you wait for me?"

"Of course," Diane said.

"You want some company?" Tyler asked.

Caroline looked as if she were about to cry. "No thanks."

When she put her hand on the door, Diane saw what the young girl had been holding. The tin soldier Brian had given her.

The door slamming sounded very loud.

"I've been having weird thoughts," Tyler said, watching the girl climb the hill toward the swampy area.

"Such as?"

"That I wish she was my daughter."

"Maybe you could adopt her."

He looked over at her. "I don't think I'm a very convincing offering as a single parent." He smiled. "Of course, if I had a wife—"

She grinned. "You don't believe in going slow, do you?"

He grinned back. "Guess I don't."

They watched Caroline against the sky on the edge of the swamp. She paused and then threw the tin soldier into the water. It disappeared beneath the tranquil waters without a trace.

When she came down the hill and got inside the car, she smelled of cold air and they could see that she was crying.

They drove in silence through a winding park. You could see pheasants against the pure midwestern sky, and in the fallen corn to the east there were fat orange pumpkins and deer.

"Could we still go to Hardees?" Caroline said in a small voice. She couldn't see the smile that passed between Diane and Tyler in the front seat.

"You bet," Diane said.

MORE GOTHIC ROMANCE
From Zebra

THE MASTER OF BRENDAN'S ISLE (1650, $2.95)
by Marion Clarke
Margaret MacNeil arrived at Brendan's Isle with a heart full of determination. But the secrets of Warwick House were as threatening as the waves that crashed upon the island's jagged rocks. There could be no turning back from the danger.

THE HOUSE OF WHISPERING ASPENS (1611, $2.95)
by Alix Ainsley
Even as the Colorado aspens whispered of danger, Maureen found herself falling in love with one of her cousins. One brother would marry while the other would murder to become master of the House of Whispering Aspens.

MIRROR OF DARKNESS (1771, $2.95)
by Monique Hara
It was an accident. She had fallen from the bluffs. Ellen's mind reeled. Her aunt was dead—and now she had no choice but to stay at Pine Cliff Manor, with the fear that her aunt's terrifying fate would be her own.

THE HOUSE AT STONEHAVEN (1239, $2.50)
by Ellouise A. Rife
Though she'd heard rumors about how her employer's first wife had died, Jo couldn't resist the magnetism of Elliot Stone. But soon she had to wonder if she was destined to become the next victim.

Available wherever paperbacks are sold, or order direct from the Publisher. Send cover price plus 50¢ per copy for mailing and handling to Zebra Books, Dept. 1862, 475 Park Avenue South, New York, N.Y. 10016. DO NOT SEND CASH.